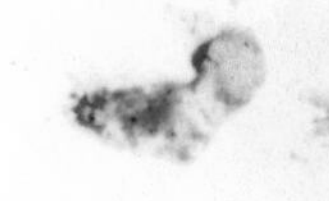

CAPTAIN AMERICA®

THE SECRET STORY OF MARVEL'S STAR-SPANGLED SUPER HERO

By David Anthony Kraft

Featuring the art of
Jack Kirby, Frank Giacoia,
and John Byrne

And the scripting of
Stan Lee and Roger Stern

CHILDRENS PRESS, CHICAGO

Library of Congress Cataloging in Publication Data

Kraft, David Anthony.
Captain America: the secret story of Marvel's star-spangled Super Hero.

Includes excerpts from the Captain America comic strip.
Summary: Discusses the origin of the comic strip character Captain America who fights against injustice and oppression, no matter what form they take.
1. Captain America (Comic strip)—Juvenile literature. [1. Captain America (Comic strip) 2. Cartoons and comics. 3. Adventure stories] I. Kirby, Jack, ill. II. Giacoia, Frank, ill. III. Byrne, John, ill. IV. Lee, Stan. V. Stern, Roger. VI. Title.
PN6728.C35K7 741.5'973 81-10020
ISBN 0-516-02411-6 AACR2

CAPTAIN AMERICA—THE MAN AND THE LEGEND!

"We shall call you Captain America . . . because, like you, America shall gain the strength and the will to safeguard our shores!"
—Dr. Reinstein
(Captain America #1, 1941)

Can there be anyone who has not heard of Captain America? It is not likely. Ask anyone. Chances are, you will find that even adults remember him—from their own childhood!

Yes, Captain America has been around for a long time. He is as vital today as he was during World War II—when he was first created. But it was that particular era that truly shaped his destiny.

It was a dark time. Clouds of war hung over Europe. The Nazi leader was Adolf Hitler (*Der Fuehrer*). He seemed to be unbeatable. His war machine left terror and destruction in its wake. Hitler was more fearsome than any comic-book villain imaginable! The world was being turned upside down. Hitler's defeat seemed impossible.

But Captain America changed that! A simple comic-book character brought hope to millions of Americans. He especially gave hope to the young American men who went to war. Captain America was the greatest. He *was* America. He gave freedom-loving people everywhere someone to look up to.

Thankfully, the Nazi menace was finally crushed. World War II did come to an end. Shortly afterward, Captain America disappeared for a while.

Then came the early 1960s. Stan Lee was spearheading the Marvel Age of Comics! The Fantastic Four! Spider-Man! The Hulk! The Avengers! A new breed of Super Hero was taking the world by storm. Stan had been a great admirer of the early Captain America tales. In fact, the first story he ever sold, when he was only fourteen, was—you guessed it—one about Captain America. Stan made a decision. It was time for Captain America to make a comeback. And what a welcome he received!

We have much more to tell you about Captain America. Later we'll tell you how he came to be. And we'll share the story of how he was discovered in modern times by the fabled Avengers. But, for now, why don't we just dive into a tale that will show Captain America in the kind of action he's famous for?

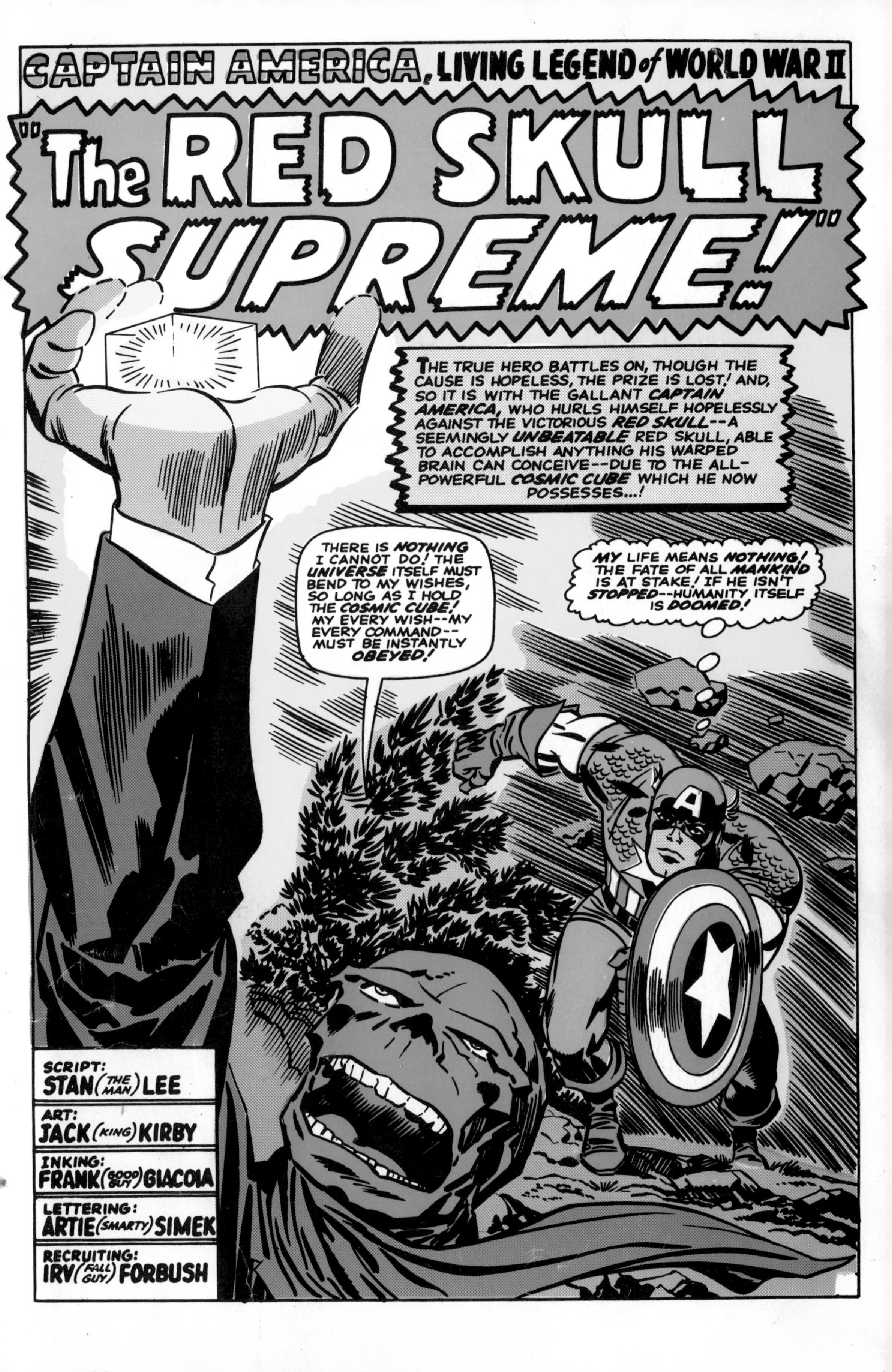
CAPTAIN AMERICA, LIVING LEGEND of WORLD WAR II
"The RED SKULL SUPREME!"
THE TRUE HERO BATTLES ON, THOUGH THE CAUSE IS HOPELESS, THE PRIZE IS LOST! AND, SO IT IS WITH THE GALLANT CAPTAIN AMERICA, WHO HURLS HIMSELF HOPELESSLY AGAINST THE VICTORIOUS RED SKULL--A SEEMINGLY UNBEATABLE RED SKULL, ABLE TO ACCOMPLISH ANYTHING HIS WARPED BRAIN CAN CONCEIVE--DUE TO THE ALL-POWERFUL COSMIC CUBE WHICH HE NOW POSSESSES...!
THERE IS NOTHING I CANNOT DO! THE UNIVERSE ITSELF MUST BEND TO MY WISHES, SO LONG AS I HOLD THE COSMIC CUBE! MY EVERY WISH--MY EVERY COMMAND--MUST BE INSTANTLY OBEYED!
MY LIFE MEANS NOTHING! THE FATE OF ALL MANKIND IS AT STAKE! IF HE ISN'T STOPPED--HUMANITY ITSELF IS DOOMED!
SCRIPT: STAN (THE MAN) LEE
ART: JACK (KING) KIRBY
INKING: FRANK (GOOD GUY) GIACOIA
LETTERING: ARTIE (SMARTY) SIMEK
RECRUITING: IRV (FALL GUY) FORBUSH

I DID IT! I REACHED HIM!
HE WAS SO WRAPPED-UP IN HIS OWN FANTASY-- SO SURE OF HIS POWER-- THAT HE ACTUALLY FORGOT ABOUT ME!
YOU UNMITIGATED FOOL!
YOU DARE ATTACK THE HOLDER OF THE COSMIC CUBE?? EVEN YOU DON'T YET COMPREHEND HOW INVINCIBLE I'VE BECOME!
BUT, YOU SHALL LEARN THAT LESSON NOW--IN A MANNER YOU'LL NEVER FORGET!
LET THE HEAT OF HADES SURROUND ME!
UNHHH! CAN'T BEAR IT! MUST BACK AWAY-- BEFORE I'M REDUCED TO A CINDER!
HAVE YOU SO SOON FORGOTTEN? ANYTHING I WISH-- ANYTHING I DESIRE-- MUST INSTANTLY COME TO PASS!
LET MY OWN HAND EMIT A SHATTERING SHOCK WAVE -- STRONG ENOUGH TO HOLD ANY FOE AT BAY!
IT'S INCONCEIVABLE! HE'S BECOME THE ULTIMATE ENEMY-- THE ULTIMATE FORCE OF EVIL!
I'VE GOT TO SEEK SHELTER-- PLAN A COUNTER-ATTACK!
THIS GIANT TREE! IF I CAN JUST-- UNHHH!
BRRAK
IT'S NO USE! HE CAUSED IT TO EXPLODE-- TO SHOWER ME WITH SHARP, DEADLY, SPEARLIKE SPLINTERS!
HE CAN MAKE A WEAPON OUT OF ANYTHING!
HAH! AT LAST YOUR DULL BRAIN BEGINS TO PERCEIVE JUST A LITTLE OF MY INCALCULABLE POWER!
BUT, WHILE YOU COWER FEARFULLY BEHIND YOUR LAMENTABLE SHIELD, I'LL GIVE YOU JUST A HINT OF THE FULL POWER WHICH IS NOW AT MY COMMAND--!

POWER ENOUGH TO AFFORD ME INSTANT DOMINATION OF THE ENTIRE HELPLESS HUMAN RACE! I HAVE BUT TO WISH IT--AND I'LL BECOME SUPREME MONARCH OF ALL OF EARTH!
THEN, BY PLACING THE COSMIC CUBE UPON MY IMPERIAL CROWN, I'LL BE ABLE TO SEND IRRESISTIBLE THOUGHT COMMANDS TO EVERY CORNER OF THE GLOBE!
"COMMANDS WHICH WILL BLANKET THE PLANET--WHICH MUST BE OBEYED BY ALL--FOR THEY SHALL BE TRANSMITTED BY THE POWER OF THE COSMIC CUBE!"
THE RED SKULL HAS GIVEN US OUR ORDERS FOR THE DAY!
WE MUST EXECUTE THEM INSTANTLY--WITHOUT HESITATION--WITHOUT QUESTION!
ALL HAIL THE IMPERIAL RED SKULL!
"I'LL TRANSFORM EVERY ABLE-BODIED MAN IN THE WORLD INTO A HUMAN FIGHTING MACHINE--WITH BUT ONE THOUGHT--ONE PURPOSE--TO DO BATTLE FOR THE RED SKULL!"
"AND THEN, WITH THE MOST POTENT FIGHTING FORCE THE UNIVERSE HAS EVER KNOWN, I'LL CREATE NEW, INVINCIBLE WEAPONS--IN ENDLESS NUMBER--WITH MATCHLESS POWER--"
"--POWER ENOUGH TO LEAVE THIS LONELY PLANET AND CARVE A NEW INTERGALACTIC EMPIRE FOR MYSELF--AN EMPIRE WHICH SHALL EXTEND TO THE FURTHEST REACHES OF SPACE!"

AND, SO LONG AS I POSSESS THE COSMIC CUBE-- NO POWER ON EARTH CAN STOP ME--LEAST OF ALL--YOU!
I CAN ERASE YOU FROM THE MEMORY OF MAN--BLOT YOU INTO UTTER NOTHINGNESS--- BY MERELY WISHING IT!
BUT, THAT WOULD BE TOO EASY-- TOO SIMPLE A FATE FOR ONE WHOM I DESPISE ABOVE ALL OTHERS!
INSTEAD, YOU SHALL MEET YOUR END IN A MORE FITTING MANNER--
--AT THE HANDS OF ONE WHO IS YOUR MASTER IN BATTLE!
YOU SHALL TASTE THE BITTER DREGS OF DEFEAT WHICH YOU HAVE SO OFTEN CAUSED OTHERS TO ENDURE! THAT IS MY COMMAND!
THUS, BEFORE YOUR VERY EYES, I CREATE AN ARTIFICIAL BEING-- POWERFUL ENOUGH TO HUMBLE YOU AT EVERY TURN!
I MUSTN'T PANIC! MUSTN'T GIVE WAY TO DESPAIR!
NO MATTER HOW AWESOME THE ODDS-- I'LL FIGHT AS I'VE LIVED--I'LL NEVER ABANDON HOPE!
SO LONG AS I REMAIN UNBEATEN-- THE SKULL'S VICTORY WILL NEVER BE ASSURED!
THE MAN-THING COMING TOWARDS ME LIKE A PUPPET-- GUIDED BY SILENT MENTAL COMMANDS...
NO MATTER HOW POWERFUL HE IS, IF I CAN OUT-THINK THE SKULL, I'LL STILL HAVE A CHANCE!
HE'LL EXPECT ME TO FEARFULLY RETREAT-- SO I'LL DO JUST THE OPPOSITE--
I'LL LAUNCH A DIRECT ATTACK, SWINGING AT HIM WITH MY SHIELD!

HAH! I ANTICIPATED THAT YOU'D TRY THAT-- BUT, MY ARTIFICIAL MAN IS FASTER THAN YOU!
SEE HOW EASILY HE DUCKED UNDER YOUR INEPT, BUMBLING ATTACK!
WHOOOOOSH!
THE SKULL IS RIGHT! HE MOVES LIKE GREASED LIGHTNING!
AND NOW, SEE HOW HE CAN STRIKE-- WITH ALL THE FORCE AND POWER I MENTALLY FEED TO HIM!
UHHHH! LUCKY I WAS ABLE TO ROLL WITH THAT ONE--OR IT WOULD HAVE FINISHED ME!
SKRAK!
HAVE TO KEEP ROLLING-- DODGING! THE SLIGHTEST SLIP WILL BE MY LAST!
BUT THEN, AS THE MAN-THING ALMOST IMPERCEPTIBLY PAUSES BETWEEN MENTAL COMMANDS...
NOW! IF I'M EVER TO COUNTER-ATTACK-- THIS IS THE TIME!
I TOOK HIM BY SURPRISE! MUSTN'T LOSE THE ADVANTAGE!
STRONG AS HE IS, I'VE A GREATER KNOWLEDGE OF LEVERAGE-- AND OF COMBAT TACTICS!

IS WITH ME! I OFF-BALANCE-- K IS ABLE TO LE HIM!
SKULL MUST ARTLED TO A NEW COMMAND! UST FINISH HIM ORE HE CAN STOP ME--!
THEN, USING EVERY IOTA OF SKILL HE POSSESSES-- APPLYING EVERY OUNCE OF RAW STRENGTH HIS STEEL-MUSCLED SINEWS CAN SUPPLY-- THE RED-WHITE-AND-BLUE AVENGER FIGHTS AS NEVER BEFORE, UNTIL--
HE'S GONE!
HE VANISHED --RIGHT BEFORE MY EYES!
OF COURSE HE'S GONE! DID YOU THINK I WOULD PERMIT ANY CREATION OF MINE TO MEET DEFEAT AT THE HANDS OF CAPTAIN AMERICA? I WISHED HIM INTO LIMBO!
BUT, AS FOR YOU-- I SHALL NEVER AGAIN MAKE THE MISTAKE OF AFFORDING YOU AN OPPORTUNITY TO FRUSTRATE MY WISHES!
THE SHEER HATRED IN HIS EYES--WHEN HE LOOKS AT ME-- LIKE NOTHING I'VE EVER SEEN BEFORE!

FAREWELL, YOU COSTUMED CLOWN! YOUR END HAS COME AT LAST!
WITH NO MORE THAN A SINGLE GESTURE--A MERE RANDOM THOUGHT--I TRANSMIT YOUR PHYSICAL ATOMS TO ANOTHER DIMENSION--
SO, THE CIRCLE IS COMPLETE! THE RED SKULL HAS WON! THE WORLD IS MINE!
I CAN'T LET IT HAPPEN! I CAN'T FAIL MY FELLOW MEN! I-I'VE GOT TO PLAY IT HIS WAY!
WAIT, SKULL--WAIT! IF YOU WANT THE GREATEST TRIUMPH OF ALL--LET ME REMAIN! LET ME SERVE YOU! THINK OF IT--THE RED SKULL--WITH CAPTAIN AMERICA AS HIS HELPLESS UNDERLING!
HMMMM--A MOST INTERESTING CONJECTURE INDEED!
AT THAT VERY SPLIT-SECOND, THE RED-MASKED MENACE HALTS THE ATOM-TRANSFERAL WITH A THOUGHT--CAUTIOUSLY STUDYING THE LIMP, MOTIONLESS FIGURE WHO SEEMS TO KNEEL HELPLESSLY BEFORE HIM--
EVERY DAY OF MY LIFE, I SHALL HAVE YOU TO GAZE UPON--TO REMIND ME HOW COMPLETE--HOW DEVASTATING MY TRIUMPH REALLY IS! YOU'LL OBEY MY EVERY COMMAND--TOADY TO MY SLIGHTEST WHIM!
WHAT OTHER CHOICE IS LEFT ME? YOU HOLD THE COSMIC CUBE!
TRUE--ALL TOO TRUE! SO LONG AS THE CUBE IS MINE, I HAVE NOTHING TO FEAR FROM YOU--OR FROM ANYONE! THEREFORE, I HAVE DECIDED--!
I SHALL FORM MY OWN VERSION OF THE KNIGHTS OF THE ROUND TABLE! THEY SHALL EXIST FOR ONLY ONE PURPOSE--TO SERVE THE RED SKULL!
AND, FOR THE MOST SUPREME IRONY--THE MOST POETIC JUSTICE--IT SHALL BE YOU WHO HEADS THEM!
YOU MEAN--YOU'D GIVE ME A CHANCE TO SERVE YOU? YOU'D ALLOW ME TO DEVOTE MY LIFE TO YOUR OWN WELFARE?
OF COURSE! THAT IS THE ONLY FITTING WAY FOR OUR EPIC BATTLE TO END! YOU'LL BE MY PERSONAL SLAVE--TILL THE END OF YOUR DAYS!
THUS HAVE I WON THE MOST MONUMENTAL VICTORY OF ALL TIME!
AND NOW, IT IS ONLY FITTING THAT I, WHO AM TRULY MASTER OF ALL, SHALL HAVE RAIMENT TO MATCH MY POWER!
THEREFORE, BY THE COSMIC CUBE I HOLD, LET ME BE CLOTHED IN A SUIT OF KINGLY, GOLDEN ARMOR!
LET ALL DEFER--TO THE RED SKULL...TO THE MATCHLESS MASTER OF MANKIND!

YOU'RE LIKE SOME SUPER-POWERFUL, PRESENT-DAY KING ARTHUR--BUT YOU'RE STRONGER BY FAR!
AND, IT WILL BE MY DESTINY TO SERVE AS YOUR FIRST KNIGHT!
HOW IT GLADDENS MY HEART TO WITNESS YOUR ABJECT SUBMISSION--YOUR FAWNING SOLICITUDE!
COME FORTH THEN, DEFEATED ONE! I SHALL PLEDGE YOU TO SERVE ME--FOR ALL THE REMAINING DAYS OF YOUR LIFE! REPEAT THE FOLLOWING OATH AFTER ME--
BEFORE YOU BEGIN, LET ME KNEEL BEFORE YOU--AS IS ONLY FITTING!
YES--FITTING INDEED--FOR SO PITIFUL A COWARD!
NOT QUITE SO, SKULL--
FITTING INSTEAD FOR ONE WHO MUST BRACE HIMSELF FOR A FINAL, DESPERATE ATTACK!!
SO LONG AS I PREVENT YOU FROM FULLY CLOSING YOUR FINGERS OVER THE CUBE, ITS POWER IS LESSENED! I'LL NEVER LET GO--UNTIL YOU DROP IT!
I-I CANNOT DESTROY YOU UNTIL I HAVE FREED MYSELF! BUT--I CAN FREE MYSELF! THE CUBE STILL POSSESSES THE POWER FOR THAT!
LET THIS ISLAND SPLIT ASUNDER! LET US BE SEPARATED IN THE HOLOCAUST! I COMMAND IT!
THAT RUMBLING SOUND! IT'S HAPPENING!
BUT--I'LL HOLD ON! NO MATTER WHAT HAPPENS--I'LL NEVER LET GO!
YOU MUST LET GO! YOU MUST!
I CAN'T BE CHEATED OF MY SUPREME TRIUMPH NOW!

BUT THEN...
CAN'T HOLD ON ANY LONGER! THE ISLE IS SPLITTING--AS HE COMMANDED! ONLY ONE CHANCE--NOW OR NEVER--!
I'VE GOT TO KNOCK THE CUBE OUT OF HIS HAND--BEFORE I LOSE HIM--!
THAK!
THE CUBE! THE CUBE!
I DID IT!
I CAN'T LOSE IT NOW!
IT MUST BE MINE! IT'S MY DESTINY!
I'M THE RED SKULL--THE MASTER OF THE WORLD! I MUST RULE--RULE!
THE MAD FOOL! HE DIVED RIGHT DOWN AMONG THE FALLING ROCKS! THEY'RE STRIKING HIM--POUNDING HIM FURTHER AND FURTHER BELOW THE SURFACE!
THE CUBE! WHERE IS IT?? I DON'T SEE THE CUBE! I CAN'T FIND IT!
BUT THEN, SECONDS LATER, GRIM REALIZATION DAWNS, AS THE ARMOR-CLAD ARCH-FIEND TRIES TO REACH THE SURFACE ONCE MORE--
AIR! MUST HAVE AIR! BUT--CAN'T RISE--CAN'T SWIM ENCASED IN ALL THIS HEAVY GOLD--!
THE WEIGHT IS FORCING ME DOWN--DOWN--

MEANWHILE, A WEARY BUT TRIUMPHANT CAPTAIN AMERICA CLINGS GRIMLY TO THE LAST REMAINING VESTIGE OF WHAT HAD ONCE BEEN THE ISLAND STRONGHOLD OF THE WORLD'S MOST DANGEROUS MENACE...
HE TALKED ABOUT IRONY--ABOUT POETIC JUSTICE--AND HE FINALLY GOT HIS WISH--
FOR, WHAT COULD BE MORE IRONIC THAN THE COSMIC CUBE--WHICH MEANT MORE THAN LIFE ITSELF TO HIM--CAUSING THE DEATH OF THE RED SKULL?
THEY BOTH VANISHED BENEATH THE WAVES--AND NEITHER IS EVER LIKELY TO BE SEEN AGAIN!
EVEN NOW, THE FANTASTIC COSMIC CUBE LIES BURIED BENEATH COUNTLESS TONS OF FALLEN ROCK--HIDDEN FOREVER FROM THE SIGHT OF MEN--
WHATEVER THE SECRET OF ITS AWESOME POWER--IT'S RETURNED TO THE BOSOM OF THE ETERNALLY ROLLING SEA--WHERE I PRAY IT WILL REMAIN--FOREVER!
AND, AS THE GALLANT GLADIATOR SILENTLY AWAITS HIS EVENTUAL RESCUE, THE MOST POWERFUL OBJECT EARTH HAS EVER KNOWN LIES HUNDREDS OF LEAGUES BENEATH HIS FEET...
AS, WITH EACH PASSING MOMENT, THE SHIFTING TIDES ROLL MORE AND MORE BITS OF UNDERSEA FLOTSAM AND JETSAM OVER THE SPOT WHERE IT SLOWLY SINKS BENEATH THE SOFT, BOTTOMLESS SAND...
UNTIL, NAUGHT REMAINS SAVE A FLEETING MEMORY--THE DREAD MEMORY OF A FATE WHICH MIGHT HAVE BEEN OURS--BUT FOR THE VALOR OF A MAN THE WORLD CALLS--CAPTAIN AMERICA!

THE RED SKULL LIVES!

Cap has fought many foes in his long career. But none of them measures up to the Red Skull. Captain America stood for America, justice, and freedom. The Red Skull, on the other hand, was a symbol of Hitler, terror, and oppression. In other words, he was a symbol of the Nazi horror. He was powerful and cunning. He answered only to Hitler himself. Eventually, he gained so much power that even Hitler couldn't control him.

At one time, the Red Skull had been a poor and mistreated street orphan. He grew up hating the world. During the Nazi occupation drives, Hitler happened to come across the youth. Something in that moment inspired Hitler. He saw the sheer hatred in the young man's eyes. Now *here* was someone Hitler could use! He had the young man taken away and specially trained. He was to become the Third Reich's greatest Super Agent.

Captain America fought the Red Skull many times during World War II. He always managed to stop the Red Skull. But he never was able to defeat this master villain completely. Decades later, it was discovered that the Red Skull still lived! Like Captain America, the Red Skull had survived in suspended animation. He was found in modern times by A.I.M., a secret criminal organization. Was this the reason fate had enabled Captain America to survive into our day? It must have been! *Someone* had to stand between the Red Skull and the free world. No matter where. No matter when. That man was Captain America, the living legend of World War II!

CAPTAIN AMERICA'S BATTLE ALBUM!

The Red Skull does tower above all others as Captain America's major foe. But Justice has many enemies. And Captain America is always ready to take up her cause.

During World War II, Captain America did not fight many Super Villains. At least, not as we think of them today. He fought Nazis. In the early years of the war, he fought on the home front against saboteurs and spies. In the later years of the war, he could be seen at all the major beachheads and battlefields.

In modern times, Captain America still fights against injustice and oppression, no matter what form they take. Today's world is not as simple as the world of the 1940s. And evil is not as open or direct as it was then. It often takes secretive forms.

Captain America has tangled with many secret spy organizations. The most sinister of these was A.I.M. (Advanced Idea Mechanics). Their goal was nothing less than total domination of the world. To reach this goal, they used the latest technology. But they failed to count on the human factor—Captain America!

Captain America has battled villains, too. Many of them had connections with evil secret organizations such as A.I.M. Captain America's strangest foe was the man called **Modok!** Modok was a mutant. He was the result of A.I.M.'s experimentation. Modok had almost unlimited power. However, he was not able to move without the aid of a special harness.

A.I.M. also came up with *adaptoids*. These were androids that could assume the human form of anyone they met. One of these became the awesome **Super-Adaptoid.** The Super-Adaptoid met the Avengers. And he gained all their powers. He then turned these powers on Captain America.

Baron Zemo is nearly as evil as the Red Skull himself. If the masked Zemo had his way, he would be the next Hitler. Zemo wants to have the world crushed and cowering at his feet. Fortunately, whenever he tries to accomplish this, Captain America is there to stop him!

Perhaps the most unusual villain Captain America ever faced was the Frenchman called **Batrok the Leaper.** Batrok was a mercenary—a soldier for hire. He was skilled in several fighting methods—especially *savate*, a French foot-boxing form. Unlike Captain America's other foes, Batrok was not truly evil. He was a swashbuckler—a free-spirited pirate. And he worked for the highest bidder. However, the more often he ran into Captain America, the greater his respect grew. He finally teamed up with Captain America. Together, they went up against Batrok's employers. Batrok has never entirely reformed—he's still kind of a pirate at heart. But he has his own peculiar code of honor—and a healthy respect for his star-spangled opponent. It is a respect that has come from much experience!

You have now been introduced to some of Captain America's greatest foes. But he has many friends as well. Foremost among these are the Avengers. They were also Cap's first friends in the modern era. It was they who discovered Captain America in suspended animation.

Here it is then—the classic tale that brought the legendary hero of World War II into the frantic and fast-paced modern world!

CAPTAIN AMERICA JOINS... THE AVENGERS!
A TALE DESTINED TO BECOME A MAGNIFICENT MILESTONE IN THE MARVEL AGE OF COMICS!
BRINGING YOU THE GREAT SUPER-HERO WHICH YOUR WONDERFUL AVALANCHE OF FAN MAIL DEMANDED!
GLORIOUSLY WRITTEN BY: STAN LEE
GRANDLY ILLUSTRATED BY: JACK KIRBY
GALLANTLY LETTERED BY ART SIMEK
STEP FORWARD, CAPTAIN AMERICA! YOUR RIGHTFUL PLACE IS HERE... AMONG THE AVENGERS!
THE MIGHTY MARVEL COMICS GROUP IS PROUD TO ANNOUNCE THAT JACK KIRBY DREW THE ORIGINAL CAPTAIN AMERICA DURING THE GOLDEN AGE OF COMICS... AND NOW HE DRAWS IT AGAIN! ALSO, STAN LEE'S FIRST SCRIPT DURING THOSE FABLED DAYS WAS CAPTAIN AMERICA-- AND NOW HE AUTHORS IT AGAIN! THUS, THE CHRONICLE OF COMICDOM TURNS FULL CIRCLE, REACHING A NEW PINNACLE OF GREATNESS!
EDITOR'S NOTE: WE SINCERELY SUGGEST YOU SAVE THIS ISSUE! WE FEEL YOU WILL TREASURE IT IN TIME TO COME!

REMEMBER THE AWESOME BATTLE BETWEEN THE HULK, SUB-MARINER, AND THE AVENGERS LAST ISSUE? AFTER THE MIGHTY HULK VANISHED, SUB-MARINER FOUND THE ODDS TOO GREAT...
WE'RE TOO LATE! HE'S GETTING AWAY!
THINKING HIMSELF BETRAYED BY THE HULK, HIS HATRED OF THE HUMAN RACE GREATER THAN EVER BEFORE, THE VENGEFUL MONARCH OF THE SEA RETURNS TO THE DEEP...
THEY HAVE WON THE FIRST BATTLE, BUT THE FINAL VICTORY WILL YET BE MINE! FOR I SHALL NEVER REST UNTIL ALL OF MANKIND PAYS THE HOMAGE WHICH IS RIGHTFULLY DUE TO NAMOR, PRINCE OF ATLANTIS!
DEEPER AND DEEPER SWIMS THE TRAGIC, ALMOST-HUMAN RULER OF THE SEA! BUT NOWHERE IN THE VAST ENDLESS DEPTHS OF THE OCEAN DOES HE FIND THE PEACE HE CRAVES!
AND NOWHERE DOES HE FIND HIS VANISHED RACE--THE PROUD, ONCE-MIGHTY HORDES OF ATLANTIS, WHO FLED FROM NAMOR WHEN THEY FELT HIS LOYALTY WAS DIVIDED BETWEEN THEM AND THE HUMANS!*
GONE--ALL GONE! WILL I EVER FIND MY PEOPLE AGAIN??
* FOR A MORE DETAILED ACCOUNT, REFER TO FANTASTIC FOUR ANNUAL #1... "SUB-MARINER VERSUS THE HUMAN RACE!" -EDITOR
TO THE TIRELESS PRINCE NAMOR, TIME AND DISTANCE ARE ALMOST MEANINGLESS, AND SO IT IS THAT WE FIND HIM, HOURS LATER, STANDING ATOP AN ICE FLOW IN THE NORTH SEA, STILL WRAPPED UP IN HIS OWN BITTER THOUGHTS...
I'LL NEVER STOP SEARCHING! I'LL NEVER FORFEIT MY BIRTHRIGHT WHILE A BREATH OF LIFE REMAINS!
BUT FINALLY, HIS DARK MUSINGS ARE INTERRUPTED, AS HE SEES...
ON THE ICE AHEAD-- A HUMAN VILLAGE! I SEE MASSES OF ACCURSED HUMANS!
AND THE KEEN-EYED NAMOR IS RIGHT! A FEW HUNDRED YARDS AWAY AN ISOLATED TRIBE OF ESKIMOS BOWS DOWN IN A STRANGE RITUAL...
OH, MIGHTY LORD OF THE FROZEN ICE, HEAR OUR PRAYERS...

THE FOOLS! THEY ARE BOWING TO A PETRIFIED FIGURE FROZEN WITHIN A CAKE OF ICE!
HEAR ME, HUMANS! THIS IS NO HELPLESS IMAGE YOU SEE BEFORE YOU! THIS IS THE SUB-MARINER, WHO HAS SWORN VENGEANCE UPON THE ENTIRE HUMAN RACE!
IT IS THE DREADED NAMOR-- THE LEGENDARY ONE!
RUN, YOU WEAK, HELPLESS MORTALS! FLEE IN TERROR BEFORE THE RIGHTFUL WRATH OF NAMOR! THUS SHALL ALL OF MANKIND ONE DAY SHRIEK IN PANIC AT THE COMING OF THE SUB-MARINER!
AND TAKE YOUR ACCURSED IDOL WITH YOU! GO-- SPREAD THE WORD-- LET THE WORLD KNOW THAT NAMOR IS STILL A FORCE TO BE RECKONED WITH!
BAH! I AM FILLED WITH SHAME! I AM DISGRACED!
HAS THE MIGHTY NAMOR BEEN REDUCED TO FIGHTING HELPLESS, FEARFUL PRIMITIVES??
HIS VERY SOUL IN A TURMOIL, THE FRUSTRATED, MADDENED SUB-MARINER LASHES OUT THOUGHTLESSLY, HEEDLESSLY, CAUSING AN AVALANCHE OF ICE IN HIS THUNDEROUS RAGE!
IS THIS ALL MY STRENGTH IS GOOD FOR?? TO LASH OUT AT UNCOMPREHENDING ESKIMOS??
RUN! FLEE THE ICE FLOE! WE MUST REACH THE TRADING POST!
THE WORLD MUST BE WARNED OF NAMOR'S RAMPAGE! THE SEA PRINCE HAS GONE MAD!
AND WHAT OF THE MYSTERIOUS FIGURE IMPRISONED WITHIN THE BLOCK OF ICE?? SILENTLY IT FLOATS AWAY... UNSEEN, UNHEARD...
...UNTIL IT HITS THE WARM WATERS OF THE GULF STREAM, WHERE THE ROCK-HARD OUTER ICE SHEATH BEGINS TO SLOWLY MELT...

UNTIL, FINALLY-- NAUGHT REMAINS BUT A FROZEN, PETRIFIED FIGURE IN A STATE OF SUSPENDED ANIMATION... A FIGURE WHICH DRIFTS PAST THE UNDERSEA CRAFT OF-- THE AVENGERS!
STOP THE ENGINES, IRON MAN! THERE IS SOMEONE OUT THERE!
LOOKS LIKE A HUMAN! BUT HOW IS IT POSSIBLE??
CAUTIOUSLY OPENING THE AIR-TIGHT ESCAPE HATCH, THE HUGE HAND OF GIANT-MAN SEIZES THE RIGID FIGURE, AND...
I'VE GOT HIM!
WHO CAN HE BE? WHY IS HE FROZEN SOLID?
LOOK! BENEATH HIS TATTERED CLOTHES-- SOME SORT OF COLORFUL COSTUME!
WAIT! DON'T YOU RECOGNIZE IT?? IT'S THE FAMOUS RED, WHITE, AND BLUE GARB OF-- CAPTAIN AMERICA!
THE WASP IS RIGHT!
CAN THIS REALLY BE THE FAMOUS SHIELD OF THE ONCE-MIGHTY CRIME-FIGHTER?
AND HIS FACE MASK -- WITH THE PROUD LETTER "A" ON IT! IT MUST BE HIM!
ALL OF YOU-- LISTEN! HE ISN'T DEAD! HE'S BREATHING! HIS EYES-- THEY'RE FLICKERING!

SUDDENLY, WITH AN EAR-SPLITTING CRY, THE POWERFUL FIGURE SPRINGS UPWARD --WITH AGONIZING SHOCK REFLECTED IN HIS EYES!
BUCKY-- BUCKY! LOOK OUT!
YOU CAN'T KILL HIM! YOU CAN'T KILL BUCKY! I WON'T LET YOU! I'LL SMASH YOU ALL!
THOR! IRON MAN! STOP HIM! HE'S GONE MAD!
BUT, AS SUDDENLY AS IT STARTED, THE LEGENDARY HERO'S WRATH SUBSIDES, AND THEN...
IT'S USELESS! I REMEMBER NOW! HE IS DEAD--HE IS! AND NOTHING ON EARTH CAN CHANGE THAT!
AND THEN, AS REALIZATION DAWNS, THE HANDSOME HEAD SLOWLY TURNS... THE CLEAR BLUE EYES TAKE IN THE AWESOME FIGURES SURROUNDING HIM...
WHERE AM I? HOW DID I GET HERE? WHO ARE YOU??
THAT'S WHAT WE WERE ABOUT TO ASK YOU!
WHO AM I??
FOR A MOMENT, I HAD ALMOST FORGOTTEN MYSELF!
BUT I AM NOT LUCKY ENOUGH TO FORGET FOREVER!
--TO FORGET THAT I WAS ONCE THE MAN THE WORLD CALLED--CAPTAIN AMERICA!

EVERYTHING FITS, EXCEPT ONE DETAIL! YOU HAVEN'T BEEN HEARD FROM SINCE THE SECOND WORLD WAR! WHY HAVEN'T YOU AGED??
I TOO HAVE PUZZLED OVER THAT FACT! HOW CAN THE TRUE CAPTAIN AMERICA STILL BE AS YOUNG AS HE WHO STANDS BEFORE US??
IF THIS IS SOME KIND OF TRICK, MISTER-- YOU'LL LIVE TO REGRET IT!
I'VE NO NEED OF TRICKS! TEST ME! TRY TO CONQUER ME!
LOOK HOW HE MANAGED TO DODGE YOUR RICHOCHETING HAMMER, THOR!
STAND BACK! I'LL GET HIM!
YOU ARE BIG, MY FRIEND --BUT IN MY DAY I FOUGHT OTHERS WHO WERE STILL BIGGER!
AND I DEFEATED THEM-- JUST AS I SHALL DEFEAT YOU!
HEY! HE'S A REAL BALL OF FIRE!
I'VE GOT TO STOP THEM, BEFORE SOMEONE GETS HURT! I'LL TAKE A GROWTH CAPSULE, FAST!
STOP! COME NO FURTHER, UNLESS YOU WANT TO STRIKE OUT AT ME, TOO!
A GIRL! BUT-- FROM WHERE--??
HAVING HALTED HIS FURIOUS ATTACK, CAPTAIN AMERICA'S FIGHTING MOOD SEEMS TO PASS, AS A VEIL OF SADNESS COMES OVER HIS EYES...
WE'RE CONVINCED, FELLOW! YOU'RE THE REAL McCOY, ALL RIGHT!
BUT WHAT HAPPENED TO YOU?? AND-- WHY HAVEN'T YOU AGED??
I FEEL WE ARE ENTITLED TO THAT EXPLANATION, CAPTAIN AMERICA!

SLOWLY, ALMOST HALTINGLY, THE INCREDIBLE TALE BEGINS TO ISSUE FORTH FROM THE LIPS OF THE MIGHTY MAN WITH THE TRAGEDY-HAUNTED EYES...
IT SEEMS LIKE ONLY YESTERDAY--BUT IT WAS MORE THAN TWENTY YEARS AGO THAT MY TEEN-AGE PAL, BUCKY--AND I--WHILE ACTING AS SECURITY GUARDS AT AN E.T.O.* ARMY BASE-- TRIED TO STOP AN EXPLOSIVE-FILLED DRONE PLANE FROM TAKING TO THE AIR!
WE'RE TOO LATE, BUCKY! WE'LL HAVE TO GO AFTER IT IN ANOTHER PLANE!
NO! DON'T STOP! I THINK I CAN REACH IT, CAP!
HAH! THUS DO I TRIUMPH OVER CAPTAIN AMERICA AND BUCKY! IF THEY REACH THE PLANE, THEY DIE! AND IF THEY FAIL, AMERICA LOSES ONE OF ITS NEWEST WEAPONS!
*E.T.O.: EUROPEAN THEATER OF OPERATIONS.
THE BOY WAS CLOSER--HE REACHED THE PLANE! BUT CAPTAIN AMERICA HIMSELF CANNOT HOLD ON!
CAN'T MAKE IT! DROP OFF INTO THE WATER, LAD! DON'T TRY TO GO IT ALONE!
NO! I CAN BRING THE PLANE BACK --I KNOW I CAN!
BUCKY! LET GO! IT MIGHT BE BOOBY-TRAPPED! YOU CAN'T DEACTIVATE THE BOMB WITHOUT ME! DROP OFF!
YOU'RE RIGHT, CAP! I SEE THE FUSE! IT'S GONNA BLOW!
"AND THOSE WERE THE LAST WORDS THAT BRAVE, WONDERFUL LAD EVER UTTERED... MAY THE LORD REST HIS SOUL!"
BUCKY!! IT EXPLODED! BUCKY'S GONE!
"AS FOR ME, I DIDN'T CARE IF I LIVED OR DIED! I STRUCK THE WATER OFF THE COAST OF NEWFOUNDLAND, AND PLUMMETTED LIKE A ROCK--WITH BUCKY'S FACE ETCHED BEFORE ME! AND THAT IS THE LAST THING I REMEMBER!"
HE'S GONE---AND I---WITH ALL MY POWER--ALL MY STRENGTH--I COULDN'T SAVE HIM!

AS FOR THE REST, BY SOME FANTASTIC STROKE OF FATE, I MUST HAVE BEEN FROZEN IN AN ICE FLOE, AND THEN FOUND BY SOME ESKIMOS WHO THOUGHT I WAS A SUPERNATURAL OBJECT! THEN, ALL THOSE YEARS, BEING IN A STATE OF FROZEN SUSPENDED ANIMATION MUST HAVE PREVENTED ME FROM AGING!
WE BELIEVE YOU, CAPTAIN AMERICA!
NOT LONG AFTERWARDS, AS THE RED, WHITE, AND BLUE-CLAD FIGURE RESTS BELOW FROM HIS GRUELLING ORDEAL...
WE HAVE REACHED OUR DESTINATION! PREPARE FOR MOORING!
SLOW DOWN, GIANT-MAN! I CAN'T MATCH THOSE BIG STRIDES OF YOURS! HMMM, LOOKS LIKE THE GENTLEMEN OF THE PRESS WERE EXPECTING US!
THEY KNOW WE WENT AFTER THE HULK!* THEY EXPECT A BIG STORY!
TOO BAD WE'LL HAVE TO DISAPPOINT THEM! WE HAD A BANG-UP FIGHT, BUT NO REAL RESULTS!
AHH, BUT WAIT TILL THEY LEARN WHO OUR PASSENGER IS, BELOW DECKS!
*SEE THE AVENGERS #3 "THE HULK AND SUB-MARINER"—ED.
THEN SUDDENLY, UNEXPECTEDLY, AT THAT VERY SPLIT-SECOND, A BLINDING FLASH TAKES PLACE --FAR BRIGHTER THAN ANY ORDINARY FLASH-BULB EXPLOSION SHOULD BE!
AND, AFTER THE SMOKE HAS CLEARED, THE AVENGERS SEEM TO BE GONE--AS IN THEIR PLACE THE CROWD SEES FOUR MOTIONLESS STONE STATUES!
HEY, PETE-- LOOK! WHAT DO YOU MAKE OF THAT?
AW, PROBABLY SOME KINDA TRICK THE AVENGERS USED TO DUCK OUT OF AN INTERVIEW!

BITTERLY DISAPPOINTED, THE REPORTERS AND PHOTOGRAPHERS RUSH OFF, TRYING TO FIND THE AVENGERS... AS THE CROWD DRIFTS AWAY TO NOTHINGNESS...
THAT'S A PRETTY CRUMMY TRICK TO PULL ON US, AFTER US WAITING ALL DAY FOR THIS INTERVIEW!
LET'S GO FIND 'EM! THEY COULDN'T HAVE GOTTEN FAR!
MINUTES LATER, THE LAST OCCUPANT OF THE UNDERSEA CRAFT SLOWLY CLIMBS UP THE HATCHWAY, HAVING BEEN AWAKENED BY THE COMMOTION ABOVE...
BUT, UPON REACHING THE SURFACE, HE FINDS...
EVERYONE'S GONE! THE PIER IS DESERTED! BUT--WHY WOULD THEY DASH OFF WITHOUT ME??
STRANGE... THOSE STATUES MUST BE IN HONOR OF THE AVENGERS! BUT THEY ARE NOT SCULPTED IN TYPICAL POSES! OH WELL, IT'S NO CONCERN OF MINE! I HAVE A WHOLE NEW WORLD TO REDISCOVER--A WORLD WHICH HAS ADVANCED TWENTY YEARS AHEAD OF ME!
HMMM, THE GIRLS ARE STILL AS LOVELY AS EVER... BUT THE FASHIONS, THE HAIRDOS... HOW DIFFERENT THEY ARE!
SALLY--LOOK! HE RESEMBLES A FIGURE I HEARD MY FATHER TALK ABOUT--A MIGHTY HERO OF YEARS AGO!
HOLY SMOKE! THAT CAN'T BE WHO I THINK IT IS!
OF COURSE! MY OLDER BROTHER TOLD ME ABOUT HIM MANY TIMES--IT WAS CAPTAIN AMERICA!
AND THE NEW YORK SKY-LINE--EVER IMPRESSIVE--EVER CHANGING! WHAT CAN THIS MAGNIFICENT STRUCTURE BE--WITH ALL THE WORLD'S FLAGS ARRAYED AROUND IT??
HEY! WATCH THE LIGHTS CROSSING THE STREET, MAC!
THE CARS HAVE CHANGED MOST OF ALL--AS THEY ALWAYS DO! WE NEVER HAD SO MANY SMALL ONES IN THE THIRTIES AND FORTIES!
WAIT! I KNOW YOU! YOU'RE--AWW, NO! IT CAN'T BE! IT'S IMPOSSIBLE!
BUT I CAN'T BE WRONG! I SAW YOU ONCE, WHEN I WAS A KID! NEVER FORGOT IT!

NO, OFFICER-- YOU'RE NOT MISTAKEN! I AM CAPTAIN AMERICA!
AND ALL THESE YEARS--ALL OF US--YOUR FANS--ALL YOUR ADMIRERS--WE THOUGHT YOU WERE DEAD! BUT YOU'VE COME BACK--JUST WHEN THE WORLD HAS NEED OF SUCH A MAN--JUST LIKE FATE PLANNED IT THIS WAY!
FORGIVE ME, CAP, WILLYA? I-I SEEM TO HAVE SOMETHING IN MY EYE!
LATER, AFTER THE OFFICER HAS DIRECTED CAPTAIN AMERICA TO A NEARBY HOTEL...
I WONDER IF THE YOUNGSTERS OF TODAY, WHO'VE GROWN UP WITH IT, REALIZE WHAT A TRULY WONDERFUL THING TELEVISION IS--TO ONE WHO HAD NEVER SEEN IT!
FINALLY, THE WEARY, LONESOME MAN DROPS OFF TO A FITFUL SLEEP...
WHAT HAPPENS NEXT?? CAN'T RETURN TO MY CAREER AS CAPTAIN AMERICA--IT WOULD BE MEANINGLESS WITHOUT BUCKY! I DON'T BELONG IN THIS AGE--IN THIS YEAR--NO PLACE FOR ME--IF ONLY BUCKY WERE HERE--IF ONLY--
THEN, SUDDENLY, HIS SUPER-KEEN SENSES DETECTING A SOFT TREAD IN THE DOORWAY, THE STARTLED BLUE EYES OPEN WIDE, AND...
BUCKY!! IT'S YOU!!
YOU'VE COME BACK!! BUCKY, YOU'VE COME BACK!!
I DON'T KNOW WHAT YOU'RE YAPPIN' ABOUT, MISTER! MY NAME'S RICK JONES, AND I'VE FOLLOWED YOUR TRAIL HALFWAY ACROSS TOWN!
THEY TELL ME YOU WERE THE LAST TO SEE THE AVENGERS--AND I GOTTA FIND THEM! SO HOW ABOUT DOIN A LITTLE TALKIN', HUH?
IT'S UNBELIEVABLE! YOU'RE LIKE HIS TWIN BROTHER! YOUR VOICE--YOUR FACE--EVERYTHING!! YOU COULD BE BUCKY'S DOUBLE!
LOOK, FELLA, YOU'RE NOT READIN' ME! ARE YOU GONNA TELL ME WHAT YOU KNOW ABOUT THE AVENGERS' DISAPPEARANCE, OR DO YOU WANT ME TO MENTION YOUR NAME TO MY PAL, THE HULK, WHEN I RUN INTO HIM AGAIN??
I DON'T KNOW WHO THE HULK IS, LAD--BUT IF THE AVENGERS ARE MISSING, I'LL BE GLAD TO HELP YOU FIND THEM!

I DIDN'T MEAN TO THROW YOU A CURVE BY CALLING YOU BUCKY! YOU SEE, HE--ONCE WAS A CLOSE FRIEND OF MINE--BUT HE'S GONE NOW! I WAS WASTING TIME--MOURNING HIM--BUT YOU'VE SUDDENLY MADE ME REALIZE THAT LIFE GOES ON! IN A WAY, BUCKY CAN STILL LIVE AGAIN!
LOOK, FELLA--AFTER WE FIND THE AVENGERS, I'M SURE THEY CAN RECOMMEND A REAL NICE HEAD SHRINKER FOR YOU!
HE THINKS I'M SOME SORT OF MADMAN! WELL, I'LL PROVE TO HIM THAT I'M NOT!
PICTURES WERE TAKEN OF THE AVENGERS AT THE DOCK! GET GOING! I WANT TO STUDY THEM!
SURE, CAP! RIGHT AWAY!
ALL OF A SUDDEN HE'S CHANGED! HE ACTS LIKE A GUY WHO'S USED TO BEING OBEYED--AND FAST!
MINUTES LATER, IN A DARKROOM BELONGING TO ONE OF RICK'S TEEN-BRIGADE MEMBERS...
THESE NEWS PICTURES SEEM ALRIGHT, BUT I'M NOT SATISFIED! CAN YOU MAKE ENLARGEMENTS?
SURE! THERE'S AN ENLARGER AROUND HERE SOMEWHERE!
AND SO...
IT'LL BE READY IN A MINUTE!
AH! THAT'S MORE LIKE IT! THAT'S WHAT I WANTED!
WHAT IS IT? I DON'T SEE ANYTHING!
WAIT--IT'S GETTING CLEARER! NOW LOOK!
NO PRESS PHOTOG'S CAMERA EVER LOOKED LIKE THAT--NOT EVEN TWENTY YEARS LATER!
IT--IT LOOKS LIKE SOME KINDA GUN!
IT'S UP TO YOU NOW, SON! IF YOU WANT TO LEARN WHAT HAPPENED TO THE AVENGERS, YOU'VE GOT TO FIND THAT MAN IN THE PICTURE!
NOW YOU'RE TALKIN' MY LANGUAGE, CAP! JUST SIT TIGHT AND WATCH MY SMOKE! I'LL ALERT MY TEEN-BRIGADE, ALL OVER THE CITY...

WITHIN AN HOUR, THE SEARCH IS ON, AS SHARP EYED TEEN-AGERS COVER THE CITY, SEEKING A PASTY-FACED MAN, WEARING OVAL SUN-GLASSES, WITH JET BLACK HAIR! NOT MUCH TO GO ON, PERHAPS, BUT STILL A STARTING POINT FOR THE EAGER BRIGADERS...
THAT'S NOT HIM! HAIR'S NOT BLACK ENOUGH!
THOUGHT I HAD HIM-- BUT HE'S MUCH TOO OLD!
WORKING AROUND THE CLOCK, THE ALERT TEEN-BRIGADE TAKES CANDID CAMERA SNAP-SHOTS OF ALL POSSIBLE SUS-PECTS, SENDING THEM IMMEDIATELY TO RICK JONES...
THAT GUY'S ANOTHER FALSE ALARM, BUT I'VE GOT A HALF-DOZEN SNAPS TO SEND RICK ANYWAY!
THEN, RACING THRU THE VAST CITY LIKE AN AVENGING STREAK, THE NIMBLE, SEEMINGLY TIRELESS CAPTAIN AMERICA FOLLOWS UP EACH LEAD, NO MATTER WHERE IT MAY TAKE HIM...
IT'S LIKE OLD TIMES AGAIN, BEING IN COSTUME--ON THE TRAIL OF SOME STRANGE, UNKNOWN MENACE!
THIS IS WHAT I WAS MEANT TO DO! THIS IS THE DESTINY I CAN NEVER ESCAPE!
AND THEN, FINALLY...
IT'S HIM! THE ONE WE'RE AFTER!
WITHOUT A MOMENT'S HESITATION, TWO HUNDRED POUNDS OF FIGHTING FURY CRASH THRU THE SHATTERING WINDOW...
BUT, IN HIS EAGERNESS, THE ATTACKING CRIME-FIGHTER HAS FAILED TO NOTICE THE GUNMEN IN THE ADJOINING ROOM--GUNMEN WHO HEAR THE CRASH AND RACE TO THE SCENE, THEIR WEAPONS THUNDERING!!
GET THAT COSTUMED CLOWN, WHO-EVER HE IS!
IT'LL BE A CINCH!

THERE'S ALWAYS THE CHANCE YOU MAY GET ME! BUT "A CINCH"? NEVER!
H-HE SLICED OUR GUNS IN TWO WITH THAT SHIELD OF HIS!
WHO IS HE, ANY-WAY??
I'VE BEEN CALLED MANY THINGS--BUT I'VE COME TO PREFER THE NAME CAPTAIN AMERICA!
I SHOULDA KNOWN! I READ ABOUT HIM WHEN I WAS A KID!
HE MUST BE A PHONY! HE'S TOO YOUNG TO BE THE REAL CAPTAIN AMERICA!
OWWW! THERE'S NO STOPPIN' HIM! HE'S LIKE A WHIRLWIND!
OOOF! IF HE'S A PHONY, I'M LITTLE RED RIDING HOOD!
NO ONE CAN PAY US ENOUGH TO FIGHT HIM! KNOCK IT OFF, MASKED MAN--WE GIVE UP!
AND THAT LEAVES YOU, FELLA! YOU'VE GOT THE KEY TO THE DISAPPEAR-ANCE OF THE AVENGERS!
BUT YOU'LL NEVER LEARN THE SECRET!
IT'S UNCANNY! HE MOVES SO FAST, MY RAY CAN'T STRIKE HIM!
THAT "GUN" YOU USED CAME FROM SOME PLACE OTHER THAN EARTH! AND SO, I SUSPECT, DID YOU! NOW TALK--WHILE YOU STILL CAN!

VERY WELL! I SEE THAT FURTHER RESISTANCE IS USELESS!
AFTER YOU HAVE HEARD MY STORY, YOU MAY FEEL PITY FOR ME, INSTEAD OF THAT RAW HATRED WHICH I SEE MIRRORED IN YOUR EYES!
I WAS RIGHT! YOU'RE NOT A HUMAN!
HOLY COW! LOOK WHAT WE'VE BEEN WORKIN' FOR! LEMME OUT OF HERE!
I'VE HAD IT! ME FOR THE STRAIGHT AND NARROW FROM NOW ON!
NOW I'LL TELL YOU WHAT I THINK! THOSE AREN'T STATUES OF THE AVENGERS! THEY ARE THE AVENGERS THEMSELVES, TURNED INTO STONE BY YOU, WHEN YOU USED YOUR RAY ON THEM WHILE POSING AS A NEWSPAPER PHOTOGRAPHER! ADMIT IT!
YES! YES! YOU'RE RIGHT! UNHAND ME! I CANNOT BEAR PHYSICAL CONTACT WITH PRIMITIVE BEINGS!
"I COME FROM A FAR DISTANT GALAXY! MY NAME WOULD BE MEANINGLESS TO YOU AS EARTH TONGUES CANNOT EVEN PRONOUNCE IT!"
"CENTURIES AGO, DUE TO ENGINE FAILURE, MY SPACE SHIP CRASHED ON EARTH, IMBEDDING ITSELF DEEP INTO THE BOTTOM OF THE SEA!"
"I MEANT EARTHLINGS NO HARM! I ROAMED YOUR PLANET, SEEKING SOMEONE TO HELP ME FREE MY SHIP! BUT THOSE I SAW FEARED ME--ATTACKED ME! IN SELF-DEFENSE I USED MY RAY GUN ON THEM, TURNING THEM TO STONE FOR ONE HUNDRED OF YOUR EARTH HOURS!"
BEHOLD! IT IS A MONSTER FROM THE NETHERWORLD! IT MUST BE SLAIN!
NO! I NEED HELP! STAY BACK --PLEASE--DON'T MAKE ME DO THIS! NO!
IT IS BEWITCHED! ONE LOOK AT IT TURNS MEN TO STONE!
YOUR HAIR--IN THE DARK, YOU MUST HAVE LOOKED LIKE A WOMAN TO THEM--AND TURNING MEN TO STONE--THAT MUST BE THE ORIGIN OF THE LEGEND OF MEDUSA! BUT--WHY DID YOU USE YOUR POWER ON THE AVENGERS??
BECAUSE OF THE ONE WHO CALLS HIMSELF SUB-MARINER! HE FOUND ME SOME DAYS AGO--TOLD ME HE WOULD FREE MY SHIP FROM THE OCEAN'S DEPTHS IF I WOULD TURN THE AVENGERS TO STONE! I-I HAD TO DO IT!

SUB-MARINER! I SEEM TO REMEMBER THAT NAME FROM THE DIM PAST! BUT TIME ENOUGH FOR HIM LATER! FIRST, YOU MUST BRING THE AVENGERS BACK TO LIFE -- AND WE WILL FREE YOUR SHIP FOR YOU!
IF ONLY YOU MEAN IT! IF ONLY I CAN BELIEVE YOU!
CAPTAIN AMERICA DOES NOT LIE! LET'S GO!
WITHIN MINUTES, THE SWASHBUCKLING ADVENTURER BRINGS THE DEFEATED ALIEN TO A WAREHOUSE WHERE THE "STATUES" HAVE BEEN STORED! THEN, FACING THE MOTIONLESS FIGURES, HE DIRECTS HIS RAY AT THEM AGAIN, AFTER FIRST REVERSING THE POLARITY!
IT'S WORKING! THEY'RE TURNING TO NORMAL!
MEANWHILE, FAR BENEATH THE SURFACE OF THE SEA, IN HIS NOW-DESERTED IMPERIAL CASTLE, A FURIOUS, FRUSTRATED PRINCE NAMOR OBSERVES THE SCENE ABOVE THRU HIS UNDERSEA SCANNER...
MY PLAN HAS FAILED! THE ONE WHO CALLS HIMSELF CAPTAIN AMERICA HAS ROBBED ME OF MY VICTORY!
BUT THIS WILL TEACH ME A LESSON! WHATEVER THE SUB-MARINER MUST DO, HE MUST DO ALONE!
I AM STILL THE MOST POWERFUL MUTANT ON EARTH -- HALF-HUMAN, HALF SEA-CREATURE! MY BRAIN IS AGILE, MY ENERGY INEXHAUSTIBLE! I MUST KEEP STRIKING UNTIL THE AVENGERS ARE DESTROYED!
AND THEN, A FICKLE FATE SEEMS TO SMILE AT NAMOR, AS HE SEES...
A TROOP OF MY ELITE GUARD! THEY HAVE NOT DESERTED ME! THEY ARE STILL SEARCHING FOR ME!
THEY SEE ME -- THEY ARE TURNING! THEY BOW IN LOYAL ACKNOWLEDGEMENT OF MY IMPERIAL PRESENCE! AND NOW -- PRINCE NAMOR IS NO LONGER ALONE!

THE NEXT DAY, THE NERVOUS ALIEN LEADS THE AVENGERS TO A REMOTE, DESERTED ISLE, AND THEN...
IT IS THERE--DIRECTLY BELOW THIS SPOT, WHERE MY SHIP IS HOPELESSLY BURIED AT THE BOTTOM OF THE SEA!
NOTHING IS HOPELESS TO THE AVENGERS, PAL! WE'LL FREE IT FOR YOU, SOMEHOW!
I FOUND IT! A HUNDRED FEET BELOW --ONLY THE TAIL SECTION IS PROTRUDING!
MINUTES LATER...
MY MUSCLES ARE TWICE NORMAL SIZE, CAP, BUT I CAN'T BUDGE IT! WE'VE GOT A JOB ON OUR HANDS!
THE ONE YOU CALL THOR ASKED ME TO POSITION THIS WATER-PROOF CLOSED-CIRCUIT TV CAMERA OVER THE HULL! I'LL RELEASE A BUOY TO HOLD IT IN PLACE!
THE CAMERA IN POSITION, THE AVENGERS SPEND THE REST OF THE AFTERNOON BUILDING A SECURE PLATFORM FOR THE THUNDER GOD TO STAND UPON...
OKAY, THOR! THIS WRAPS IT UP! WHAT'S THE NEXT MOVE?
WELL DONE! NOW STAND BACK, MY FRIENDS! A POWER GREATER THAN ANY OF YOU HAVE EVER WITNESSED IS ABOUT TO BE UNLEASHED UPON THIS SPOT!
AND NOW...
SIGHTING UPON THE ENTRAPPED SPACE SHIP THRU HIS TV VIEWER, THE MIGHTY THOR SLOWLY ROTATES HIS ENCHANTED HAMMER OVER THE HULL, DIRECTING AN IRRESISTIBLE TORRENT OF COSMIC MAGNETIC WAVES TOWARD THE ALIEN CRAFT!
STEADILY, WITH EVER-INCREASING FORCE, THEY PULL AT THE HEAVY OBJECT--WITHOUT LET-UP, WITHOUT EVER SLACKENING--UNTIL--
WHOOOM!

NOT UNTIL LATER WILL THE IRONY OF THE SITUATION DAWN UPON THE FRUSTRATED SEA PRINCE! FOR, THE VERY ALIEN HE HAD HOPED WOULD DESTROY THE AVENGERS, HAS UNWITTINGLY RESCUED THEM AT THE CRUCIAL MOMENT!
IT'S THE ALIEN! HE'S RETURNING TO THE STARS!
THE WATERS HAVE SUBSIDED! THE ISLAND IS STILL INTACT!
BUT NAMOR IS GONE--AND SO IS OUR CHANCE TO DEFEAT HIM!
EASY, LAD! IT'S ALL OVER! YOU'RE SAFE NOW!
I NOTICE IT TOOK A THREAT TO THE BOY TO BRING YOU INTO ACTION, FELLA!
THOUGH NAMOR IS GONE, I FEEL WE SHALL MEET HIM AGAIN--IN MORTAL COMBAT! BUT, ONE OF US IS STILL NOT PRESENT!
I THOUGHT YOU'D NEVER NOTICE, BLUE-EYES!
I WAS DOING WHAT ANY GIRL WOULD DO IN A MOMENT OF CRISES--POWDERING MY NOSE, OF COURSE!
ONLY ONE THING PUZZLES ME --WHEN I WRITE THIS DOWN IN MY DIARY, DO I CALL IT A VICTORY--OR A DEFEAT??
THAT'S FOR HISTORY TO DECIDE, HON! RIGHT NOW, WE'VE ANOTHER DECISION TO AWAIT...
RIGHT! WE HAVE AN OFFER TO PROPOSE TO CAPTAIN AMERICA!
I HAVE SEEN YOU IN BATTLE --AND THERE ARE NONE BRAVER! IF YOUR OFFER IS WHAT I HOPE IT IS, MY ANSWER IS YES!
SPOKEN WITH HONOR, AND WITH DIGNITY, LIKE A MAN!
THUS, WE ARE PRIVILEGED TO WITNESS A MOMENTOUS MOMENT IN THE ANNALS OF HIGH ADVENTURE...
WE WELCOME YOU, CAPTAIN AMERICA, TO THE RANKS OF-- THE AVENGERS!
23
BUT, THERE IS ONE WHOSE HEART IS STILL HEAVY--STILL FILLED WITH A DREAD FEAR--
HE'S THE GREATEST GUY I EVER MET--AND I CAN TELL HE WANTS ME TO BE HIS PARTNER! BUT WHAT ABOUT--THE HULK??
HE'S SURE TO RETURN SOME DAY... AND WHEN HE FINDS OUT THAT CAPTAIN AMERICA HAS REPLACED HIM--WILL ANYTHING BE ABLE TO STOP HIM THEN??!
BUT, NOTHING IN LIFE IS CERTAIN! AND WE MUST TAKE THE GOOD AND THE BAD AS FATE DEALS THEM OUT! ONE THING IS CERTAIN, THOUGH-- NEXT ISSUE OF THE AVENGERS WILL HAVE MORE SUPER-HEROES, SUPER-VILLAINS, AND SUPER-THRILLS--JUST AS YOU WANT THEM!

Sure enough! Many more Super Heroes, Super Villains, and awesome adventures have followed. Captain America has survived many trials. Every one has added to his legend!

It has not been easy for him to make the change from the wartime 1940s to our modern era. But Captain America has met the challenge. Along the way he has had the help of a few close friends and famous partners.

None were ever as close as **Bucky Barnes**, the partner who was tragically killed at the end of World War II. Bucky was like a son to Captain America. But both of them knew the risks they were taking. They also knew what was at stake—the future of free men everywhere!

Captain America is still fighting for freedom and justice wherever there is a need. And many are those who stand tall to fight beside him.

THE AVENGERS—EARTH'S MIGHTIEST HEROES!

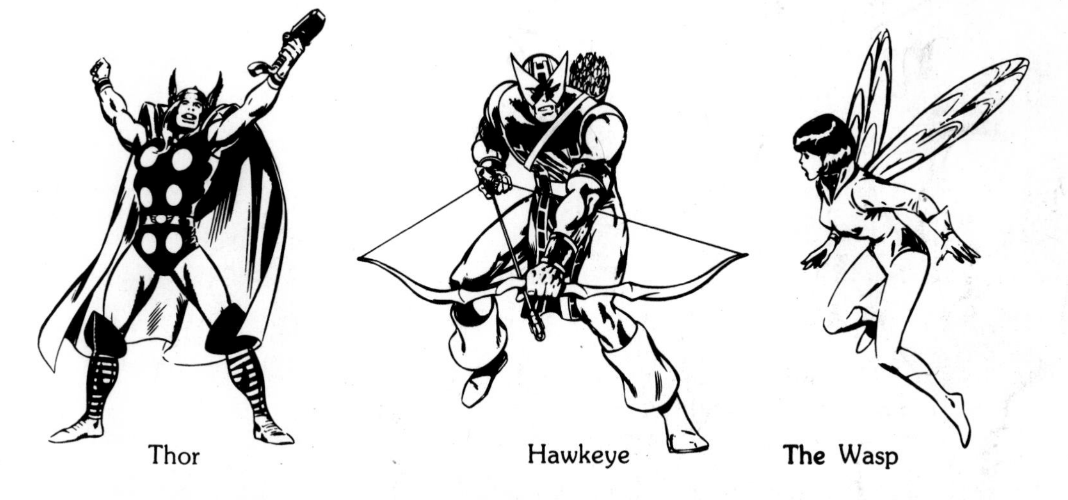

Thor Hawkeye The Wasp

Captain America has been with the Avengers ever since they first discovered him, frozen, in the ocean. He has seen the membership of the group change many times. He quickly earned the respect of the Avengers and soon became their leader. It has given him an awesome

The Avengers

responsibility. But it also has given him companionship. Without the Avengers, Captain America might have had a very lonely comeback. And who wouldn't be proud to lead such as these into battle: Iron Man, Thor, Hawkeye, the Scarlet Witch, Vision, the Wasp, and Wonder Man?

You will remember that we mentioned secret organizations for evil. A.I.M. was only one such organization. But the free world also has a powerful secret organization. This organization fights for justice. It is called S.H.I.E.L.D.—Supreme Headquarters International Espionage Law-enforcement Division. Captain America often works with this organization. Its director, Nick Fury, and his top agent, "Dum Dum" Dugan, are two of Captain America's closest friends. When all three take on a mission together—hoo boy!—we start feeling sorry for the villains!

Captain America was close to one other agent of S.H.I.E.L.D. She was called Agent 13. Her name was Sharon Carter. Captain America and Agent 13 fell in love. But both had sworn to wage war on evil. And neither could give that up. Eventually, Agent 13 was killed in the line of duty.

One man was nearly as close to Captain America as Bucky Barnes. That was Sam Wilson—the **Falcon**. Along with Redwing, his fantastic trained falcon, Sam Wilson fought side-by-side with Captain America for several years. And, once more, Captain America almost lost a partner. Almost!

Redwing

The Falcon

In their greatest battle together, the Red Skull took control of Sam Wilson's personality. He made Captain America believe that Sam was a criminal. Cap and Sam did finally defeat the Red Skull. Even so, it took many months to sort out Sam Wilson's identity. When the adventure was finally over, Sam decided he needed some time to get away and relax. Chances are very good, however, that the world has not heard the last of the high-flying Falcon!

THE BIRTH OF A LEGEND!

You have met Captain America. You have seen his many powerful friends and villainous foes. You have seen Captain America in all-out action—the kind that made him the legend of two eras. It is now time to journey back, back to the beginning. It is time to learn how the legend was born!

By the end of the 1930s, the Nazi war machine was already rolling. Still, the governments of the world did not yet understand the threat completely. But one group did pay attention. And these were people who were not afraid to speak out. They were the creative people—writers, artists, and filmmakers. They saw the atmosphere of oppression gripping Europe like an iron glove. They began to find creative ways to make Americans aware of the tragedy that was sure to come.

Two men working in the comics field found a special way to do this. They were Joe Simon and Jack Kirby. These two original thinkers produced a symbol that all America would be proud to stand behind. They produced Captain America!

Following is a fine retelling of the original story of how Captain America came to be. It is a modern retelling, but it captures the flavor of the 1940s.

Prepare yourself—you are about to witness *history*!

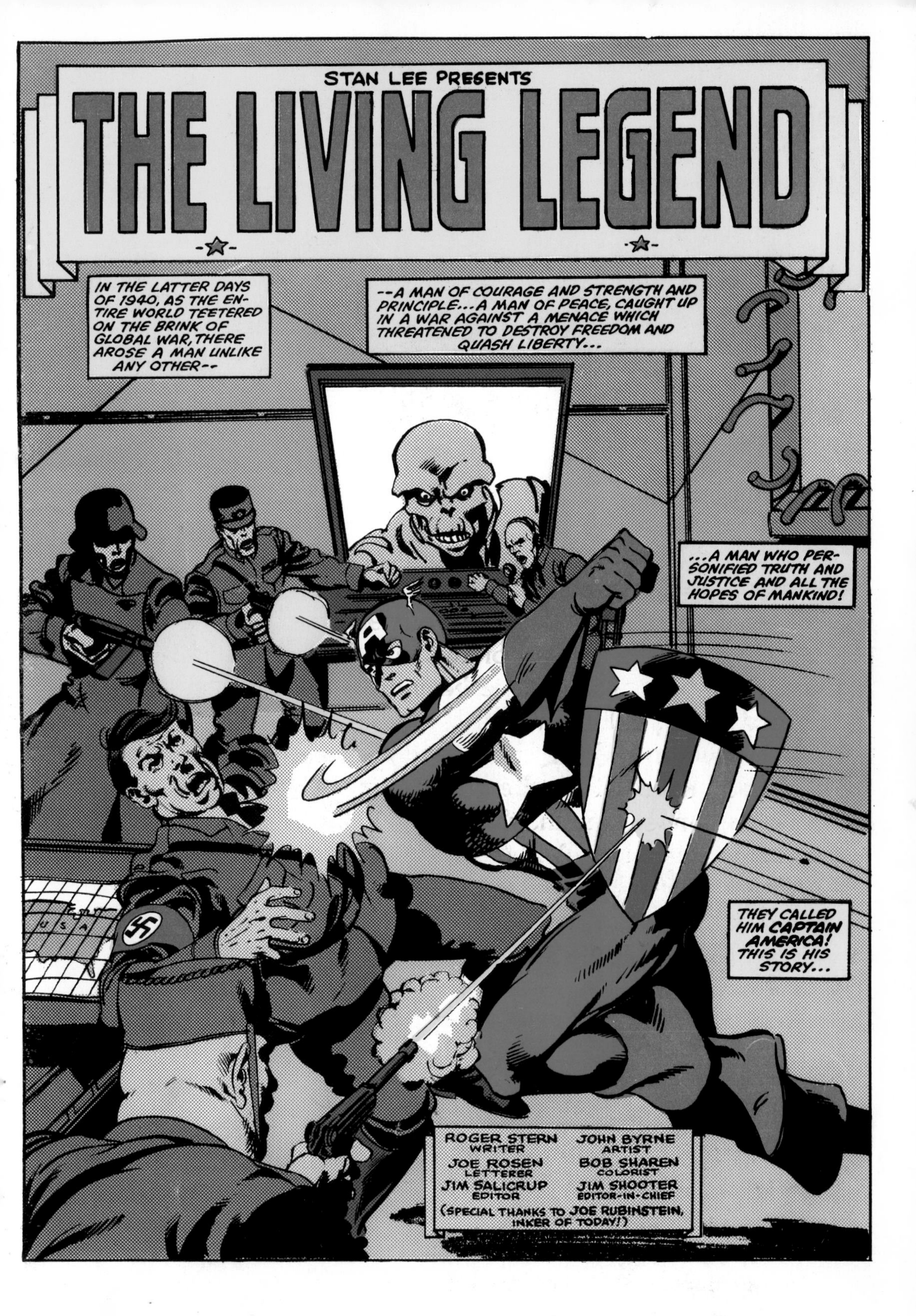
STAN LEE PRESENTS
THE LIVING LEGEND
IN THE LATTER DAYS OF 1940, AS THE ENTIRE WORLD TEETERED ON THE BRINK OF GLOBAL WAR, THERE AROSE A MAN UNLIKE ANY OTHER--
--A MAN OF COURAGE AND STRENGTH AND PRINCIPLE... A MAN OF PEACE, CAUGHT UP IN A WAR AGAINST A MENACE WHICH THREATENED TO DESTROY FREEDOM AND QUASH LIBERTY...
...A MAN WHO PERSONIFIED TRUTH AND JUSTICE AND ALL THE HOPES OF MANKIND!
THEY CALLED HIM CAPTAIN AMERICA! THIS IS HIS STORY...
ROGER STERN WRITER
JOHN BYRNE ARTIST
JOE ROSEN LETTERER
BOB SHAREN COLORIST
JIM SALICRUP EDITOR
JIM SHOOTER EDITOR-IN-CHIEF
(SPECIAL THANKS TO JOE RUBINSTEIN, INKER OF TODAY!)

JUNE, 1941... WASHINGTON, D.C.
IN THE OVAL OFFICE OF THE WHITE HOUSE, PRESIDENT FRANKLIN DELANO ROOSEVELT HAS CANCELED ALL APPOINTMENTS, FORCING CONGRESSMEN AND V.I.P.'S ALIKE TO WAIT WHILE HE RECEIVES A VERY NON-DESCRIPT VISITOR...
...A YOUNG COURIER FROM G-2, THE INTELLIGENCE ARM OF THE DEPARTMENT OF THE ARMY.
WELL, SON, LET'S GET ON WITH IT! I HAVE THE EDITOR OF THE WASHINGTON POST COOLING HIS HEELS OUTSIDE-- AND I'M SURE I'LL HEAR ABOUT IT IN TOMORROW'S HEADLINES!
YES, SIR... I'M SORRY, SIR!
OH, THAT'S ALL RIGHT! I'VE DEVELOPED A FAIRLY THICK SKIN AS FAR AS BAD PRESS IS CONCERNED!
YES, SIR. AS PER YOUR REQUEST, THIS IS THE FULL AND COMPLETE DOSSIER ON OPERATION: REBIRTH!
THIS IS IT?
YOU KNOW, SON, SOMETIMES I DESPAIR. THIS WAS ONE OF THE MOST AMBITIOUS TOP-SECRET PROJECTS IN THE NATION'S HISTORY...
OPERATION: REBIRTH
...AND IT CAME TO SUCH A TRAGIC END! BUT, I WANTED TO LEARN MORE ABOUT REBIRTH'S TEST SUBJECT... THIS YOUNG LAD, STEVE ROGERS. HMM... I SEE HERE--
"--THAT HE GREW UP ON THE LOWER EAST SIDE OF NEW YORK CITY! EVIDENTLY, MUCH OF HIS YOUTH WAS SPENT--
OPERATION: REBIRTH
"--TRYING TO HELP HIS FAMILY MAKE ENDS MEET DURING THE DEPTHS OF THE DEPRESSION. OH... I SEE...
"...HIS FATHER DIED WHEN HE WAS STILL A CHILD, AND HIS MOTHER HAD TO STRUGGLE JUST TO KEEP HER SON AND HERSELF FED.
"STILL, DESPITE THEIR DEPRIVATION, STEVE KEPT UP WITH HIS SCHOOLING, AND BECAME A VORACIOUS READER... ESPECIALLY OF FANTASY!
"GIVEN THE STATE OF HIS REALITY, I CAN WELL UNDERSTAND WHY!"
"AH, IT SEEMS THAT THE BOY ALSO HAD A NATURAL TALENT FOR ART. BUT HE KEPT HIS LOVE OF ART, AND OF BOOKS, A SECRET TO AVOID TAUNTS AND BEATINGS AT THE HANDS OF HIS PEERS.

"AS THE DEPRESSION WORE ON, TIMES BECAME INCREASINGLY DIFFICULT FOR THE ROGERS' HOUSEHOLD. SARAH ROGERS TOOK IN LAUNDRY... AND TAXED HERSELF TO THE LIMIT TO PROVIDE FOR HER SON.
"BUT TIME AND HARDSHIP EVENTUALLY TOOK ITS TOLL, AND AS STEVEN ENTERED HIS LATE TEENS, HIS MOTHER PASSED ON--
"--A VICTIM OF PNEUMONIA.
"OUT ON HIS OWN, YOUNG ROGERS MANAGED TO FIND A CHEAP BOARDING HOUSE AND TOOK A JOB AS A DELIVERY BOY. IT WAS NOT AN EASY LIFE, NOR A VERY GOOD ONE...
"...BUT SOMEHOW, HE SURVIVED.
"AND THEN, ONE DAY, WHILE TRYING TO ESCAPE INTO THE FANTASY WORLD OF THE MOVIES, STEVE ROGERS ENCOUNTERED AN EVEN HARSHER REALITY--
"--IN NEWSREEL FOOTAGE OF THE NAZI WAR MACHINE IN ITS RELENTLESS MARCH ACROSS A WAR-TORN EUROPE!"
THOSE NEWSREELS... IT'S AWFUL... AWFUL! IT'S AS IF HALF THE WORLD HAS GONE MAD!
THE SEA HAWK
ERROL FLYNN
NEWS
PAPERS
TOBBACC
IF THE NAZIS AREN'T STOPPED SOON, THERE WON'T BE A FREE MAN LEFT ALIVE ANYWHERE! I HAVE TO DO SOMETHING... I HAVE TO!
"HOWEVER..."
SON, ARE YOU SURE YOU'VE BEEN CLASSIFIED 1-A?
NO, SIR! THEY WOULDN'T DRAFT ME! THAT'S WHY I'M VOLUNTEERING! I HATE WAR AND SENSELESS BLOODSHED, BUT I KNOW WHAT THE NAZIS ARE DOING IN EUROPE.
IT'S JUST A MATTER OF TIME BEFORE THE UNITED STATES IS INVOLVED IN THE WAR, AND I CAN'T STAY BEHIND WHILE OTHERS DO THE FIGHTING!
I'M SORRY, SON, BUT YOU'RE MUCH TOO FRAIL FOR MILITARY SERVICE!
BUT YOU JUST HAVE TO PASS ME! THERE MUST BE SOMETHING I CAN DO!
I COULDN'T HELP OVERHEARING, SON. I'M GENERAL PHILLIPS... ARE YOU REALLY SERIOUS ABOUT WANTING TO TAKE PART IN THE BIG PICTURE?
I AM, SIR! I'LL DO ANYTHING--ANYTHING!

"IT MUST HAVE BEEN KISMET! IN STEVE ROGERS, GENERAL PHILLIPS HAD FOUND THE IDEAL TEST SUBJECT FOR OPERATION: REBIRTH.
"WITHIN MINUTES, ROGERS WAS ON A PLANE, SPEEDING TOWARDS WASHINGTON. AND, AS NIGHT FELL, HE WAS TAKEN TO A SMALL CURIO SHOP ON A LITTLE-KNOWN CAPITAL SIDE STREET.
ANTIQUES and COLLECTABLES
"I CAN WELL IMAGINE THE SURPRISE ROGERS FELT UPON ENTERING THAT MOLDERING OLD STOREFRONT..."
HALT! IDENTIFY YOURSELVES OR DIE!
AGENTS L-7 AND X-9 REPORTING, AGENT R! THE PASSWORD IS "EAGLE!"
WE HAVE "THE VISITOR" WITH US.
ENTER AND LOCK THE DOOR BEHIND YOU!
I-I DON'T GET IT! HOW CAN SUCH AN IMPORTANT PROJECT BE HOUSED IN A SMALL SHOP LIKE THIS? NOTHING I'VE SEEN SO FAR SEEMS TO MAKE SENSE!
IN WORK SUCH AS OURS, THINGS ARE SELDOM WHAT THEY SEEM.
WHY... YOU... YOU'RE NOT--! THAT IS... I THOUGHT--!
FORGIVE THE THEATRICS. I ASSURE YOU, THEY ARE QUITE NECESSARY.
"IT MUST HAVE BEEN A NIGHT FULL OF SURPRISES FOR OUR YOUNG 'VISITOR.' AS AGENT R STOOD GUARD, ROGERS WAS CONDUCTED UP A NARROW FLIGHT OF STAIRS, THROUGH A HIDDEN DOORWAY, AND INTO ONE OF THE MOST ADVANCED BIOCHEMICAL LABORATORIES IN THE FREE WORLD."
IT... IT'S AMAZING! LIKE SOMETHING OUT OF H.G. WELLS!
GET USED TO IT, ROGERS. YOU'RE GOING TO BE SPENDING SOME TIME HERE.
"AND THEN..."
WELCOME TO OPERATION: REBIRTH, MR. ROGERS. I'M DR. ANDERSON, THE DIRECTOR OF PROJECTS... AND THIS IS OUR HEAD SCIENTIST, PROFESSOR REINSTEIN!
REINSTEIN? WHY, THAT'S DR. ABRAHAM ERSKINE, THE FAMOUS BIOCHEMIST!
BUT I THOUGHT HE'D DIED LAST SPRING IN AN AUTO CRASH!
THAT IS WHAT WE WANTED THE WORLD TO BELIEVE, MY BOY!
IT LOOKS LIKE THE SECURITY BOYS WERE RIGHT TO KEEP YOU UNDER WRAPS, ABRAHAM. YOUR FACE IS TOO RECOGNIZABLE... THE REINSTEIN CODE-NAME DIDN'T FOOL YOUNG ROGERS FOR A MINUTE!
STEVEN, WE HAVE TO LEVEL WITH YOU... OUR EXPERIMENT MIGHT GIVE YOU A STRONG NEW BODY. BUT IT MIGHT KILL YOU!
I'M WILLING TO FACE THOSE CONSEQUENCES, SIR.
VERY WELL, THEN... WE SHALL BEGIN OUR WORK AT ONCE!

"OVER THE NEXT FEW WEEKS, ROGERS WAS PUT THROUGH A GRUELING SERIES OF TESTS TO DETERMINE THE EXACT LIMITS OF HIS PHYSICAL ABILITIES -- WHILE DR. ERSKINE WORKED ON HIS SECRET TISSUE-BUILDING SERUM!
"AND THEN, THAT DAY ARRIVED WHEN ANDERSON BURST IN ON THE GENERAL AND MYSELF WITH THE NEWS..."
THE CHEMICAL IS PERFECTED, GENTLEMEN -- AND I SUGGEST THAT WE PROCEED AT ONCE!
THEN THE TIME HAS COME AT LAST!
THERE IS NOTHING MORE TO BE SAID. I WISH YOU ALL GOD-SPEED!
"CHANGING TO CIVILIAN CLOTHING, GENERAL PHILLIPS AND UNDER-SECRETARY SIMMS WERE CONDUCTED TO THE HIDDEN LABORATORY BY DR. ANDERSON HIMSELF.
"AND WHEN THEY ARRIVED, A MAN WHOSE CREDENTIALS IDENTIFIED HIM AS SPECIAL AGENT CLEMSON WAS ALREADY THERE...
"...WAITING!"
"AND, WHILE THE DIGNITARIES ASSEMBLED IN THE OBSERVATION CHAMBER, TWO ROOMS AWAY, DR. ERSKINE WAS MAKING SOME FINAL PREPARATIONS."
STEVEN, MY BOY, ONCE I INJECT YOU WITH THE DILUTE SOLUTION OF MY SERUM, THERE CAN BE NO TURNING BACK!
I... WOULD NOT BLAME YOU IF YOU WISHED TO BACK OUT NOW. THIS COULD COST YOU YOUR LIFE!
SIR, GOOD MEN FROM POLAND TO GREAT BRITAIN HAVE BEEN PUTTING THEIR LIVES ON THE LINE. CAN I DO ANY LESS?
LET'S GET ON WITH IT!
I BELIEVE YOU ARE THE BRAVEST YOUNG MAN I HAVE EVER MET!
THIS WILL STING FOR JUST A MOMENT, THEN YOU WILL FEEL A SLIGHT DIZZINESS.
"THEN, ERSKINE LED HIS SUBJECT INTO THE MAIN LABORATORY..."
GENTLEMEN, THIS DISTINGUISHED YOUNG VOLUNTEER HAS ALREADY BEEN INJECTED WITH MY SECRET SERUM--
--HE IS NOW READY TO TAKE THE ORAL FORM OF THE COMPOUND!
YOU MUST DRINK THIS QUICKLY, BEFORE THE CHEMICALS LOSE THEIR POTENCY. GOOD LUCK, MY BOY!

GENTLEMEN, IF WE HAVE ERRED, ROGERS WILL BE DEAD WITHIN SECONDS, FOR HE IS DRINKING THE STRONGEST CHEMICAL POTION YET CREATED BY MAN!
BUT, IF WE SUCCEED, IF HE LIVES, HE WILL BE THE FIRST OF AN ARMY OF FIGHTING MEN SUCH AS THE WORLD HAS NEVER SEEN!
HIS REFLEXES, HIS PHYSICAL CONDITION WILL BE SECOND TO NONE! AND HIS COURAGE...
...WELL HIS COURAGE HAS ALREADY BEEN PROVEN!
NOW, YOU SHALL SEE HOW I SPEED UP THE SERUM'S PROCESS--AND HOW IT WILL AFFECT ROGERS' BODY TISSUE!
OBSERVE! I AM BOMBARDING HIS BODY WITH POTENT, INVISIBLE VITA-RAYS!
ONCE THE PROCESS IS COMPLETED, THE FRAIL YOUNG MAN WHO STOOD BEFORE YOU WILL BE FRAIL AND SICKLY NO LONGER!
INSTEAD, HIS EVERY BODY CELL WILL SURGE WITH NEW POWER, NEW VIGOR, NEW VITALITY!
YAARRGH!
E-EVERYTHING IS SPINNING AROUND! I... FEEL LIKE I'M BLACKING OUT... BUT... I... MUST... HANG ON!
IT'S WORKING! DON'T GIVE UP, SON! HOLD ON! THIS IS THE MOMENT OF CRISIS! YOU MUST SURVIVE IT!
I... I CAN FEEL POWER SURGING THROUGH ME! MY BODY'S GETTING LARGER --STRONGER!
IT'S AS IF MILLIONS OF CELLS WERE FORMING AT INCREDIBLE SPEED!
IN A MATTER OF MINUTES--I'VE ACTUALLY BECOME A NEW MAN!

I... I HAD HOPED IT WOULD WORK, BUT I NEVER IMAGINED IT WOULD BE... LIKE THIS! IT'S... A MIRACLE!
YES, A MIRACLE OF SCIENCE! THINK WHAT THIS WILL MEAN TO OUR NATION! THINK WHAT IT CAN ONE DAY MEAN TO THE WORLD! MY SERUM WILL VIRTUALLY WIPE OUT DISEASE... WEAKNESS... INFIRMITY!
STEVEN, YOU HAVE BECOME A NEARLY PERFECT HUMAN BEING!
ANDERSON, THIS IS PHENOMENAL! WE MUST GET THE SERUM MASS-PRODUCED AT ONCE!
"BUT THEN, IN THE MIDST OF SUCCESS, TRAGEDY STRUCK!"
NO! ERSKINE AND HIS ACCURSED EXPERIMENT SHALL BOTH DIE IN THAT ROOM!
KRAK
NONE SHALL LIVE TO OPPOSE THE FUEHRER'S THIRD REICH!
STEVEN... MY FORMULA, MY PROCESS CAN NEVER BE TOTALLY DUPLICATED!
BUT YOU... YOU STILL LIVE! YOU... MUST ALWAYS BE WORTHY!
DR. ERSKINE!
IT... IT'S TOO LATE! HE'S GONE!
CRASH
YOU! YOU'RE THE ONE WHO DID THIS! YOU'RE THE ONE WHO FIRED THE SHOT!
I WAS TO BE THE FIRST. BUT NOW THERE ARE NONE BUT ME TO PERPETUATE DR. ERSKINE'S DREAM!
AS LONG AS I LIVE, I'LL DEDICATE MYSELF TO THE CAUSE OF FREEDOM--TO DESTROY THE ENEMIES OF LIBERTY!
BAH! LIKE ALL FREEDOM-LOVING FOOLS, YOU ONLY TALK, WHILE WE NAZIS ACT!
NOW YOU SHALL SHARE THE DOCTOR'S FATE!
NO! YOU'LL NOT STOP ME NOW! I SHALL FIGHT--I MUST FIGHT--FOR ALL THOSE WHO MIGHT HAVE BEEN!

"IN A MATTER OF MINUTES, THE GLEAMING HOPE OF OPERATION: REBIRTH CAME TO AN ABRUPT END.
"THE SECRET OF THE SUPER-SOLDIER SERUM APPARENTLY DIED WITH DR. ERSKINE, WHO HAD NEVER COMMITTED THE FULL FORMULA TO PAPER.
"AS FOR 'AGENT CLEMSON,' A MAN WE LATER IDENTIFIED AS NAZI ASSASSIN HEINZ KRUGER... HE, TOO, PAID THE FINAL PRICE.
"KNOCKED INTO THE VITA-RAY DEVICE'S ELECTRICAL OMNI-VERTER POWER SOURCE BY ROGERS' PUNCH, HE SCRAMBLED TO FREE HIMSELF--
"--AND IN DOING SO, HE GRABBED HOLD OF THE OMNI-VERTER'S HIGH-VOLTAGE TERMINALS ...AND WAS INSTANTLY ELECTROCUTED!
"THE SUPER-SOLDIER SERUM WORKED... ROGERS WAS LIVING PROOF OF THAT! BUT WE COULD NEVER PRODUCE ANOTHER MAN LIKE HIM..."
...AND SO ENDED OUR BOLD EXPERIMENT.
THE WORLD IS POORER FOR THE LOSS OF ABRAHAM ERSKINE!
YES, SIR. BUT HE DID LEAVE US AN IMPORTANT LEGACY--
--IN THE "REBORN" STEVE ROGERS. AS YOU KNOW, ACTING UPON GENERAL PHILLIPS ADVISEMENT, ROGERS BECAME THE CORNERSTONE OF... PROJECT: SUPER-SOLDIER!
AS THIS DOSSIER SHOWS, MR. PRESIDENT--
PROJECT: SUPER-SOLDIER
TOP SECRET
"--SHORTLY AFTER DR. ERSKINE'S TRAGIC DEATH, ROGERS WAS PUT INTO A SPECIAL TRAINING PROGRAM, TO TEACH HIM HOW TO BEST USE HIS NEW BODY!
"FOR THREE MONTHS, HE WORKED OUT WITH THE GREATEST BOXERS, WRESTLERS, BODY BUILDERS, AND GYMNASTS THE FREE WORLD HAD TO OFFER! AND WHATEVER TIME NOT SPENT IN PHYSICAL TRAINING WAS SPENT IN LEARNING THE FINE POINTS OF MILITARY STRATEGY AND TACTICS.
"THIS WAS PERSONALLY SUPERVISED BY GENERAL PHILLIPS!

"AND THEN, IN MARCH OF THIS YEAR..."
WELL, STEVE, I SUPPOSE YOU'VE BEEN WONDERING JUST WHAT WE'VE HAD IN MIND FOR YOU... WHAT WITH ALL OF THIS TRAINING.
I ASSUMED THAT YOU WERE GROOMING ME FOR SOME SORT OF TOP-SECRET SPECIAL MISSION, SIR.
YES, A VERY SPECIAL MISSION! YOU SEE, THE NAZIS HAVE A SPECIAL AGENT WHO IS CURRENTLY SPREADING TERROR ACROSS THE FACE OF EUROPE!
HE'S CALLED... THE RED SKULL! AND IT'S RUMORED THAT SOME MEMBERS OF THE NAZI HIGH COMMAND FEAR HIM EVEN MORE THAN THEY DO HITLER!
THE SKULL HAS COME TO PERSONIFY THE EVIL OF NAZISM. WE DESPERATELY NEED AN AGENT WHO IS HIS OPPOSITE... A MAN WHO WILL BE A LIVING SYMBOL OF LIFE AND LIBERTY!
AND... YOU WANT ME TO BE THAT MAN?
YES, STEVE... WE DO. IN THIS PACKAGE, YOU'LL FIND A UNIFORM SPECIALLY DESIGNED FOR YOU... TRY IT ON!
I... REALIZE THAT THIS IS AN AWESOME RESPONSIBILITY, STEVE. YOU'RE BEING ASKED TO REPRESENT AMERICA, TO BOTH HER PEOPLE AND THE WORLD.
BUT WE NEED YOU TO INSPIRE THE PUBLIC... TO GIVE THEM HOPE THROUGH THE DARK DAYS THAT LIE AHEAD.
THEN I PRAY THAT I'M EQUAL TO THE TASK, GENERAL! THIS LAND OF OURS MAY HAVE SEEN SOME HARD TIMES, AND MAYBE IT HASN'T ALWAYS LIVED UP TO THE PROMISE OF THE FOUNDING FATHERS...
...BUT AMERICA AT ITS BEST HAS ALWAYS STOOD FOR THE RIGHTS OF MAN, AND AGAINST THE RULE OF TYRANTS!
AND IF AMERICA NEEDS A MAN TO STAND FOR HER PRINCIPLES, TO BATTLE THE FORCES OF TYRANNY--THEN, AS GOD IS MY WITNESS, I SHALL BE THAT MAN!

"ROGERS GOT HIS FIRST CHANCE TO LIVE UP TO THAT PLEDGE JUST THREE NIGHTS LATER...WHEN, ON A DESERTED BACK ROAD IN THE MARYLAND COUNTRYSIDE--
"--AS A HIGH-RANKING COLONEL WAS BEING DRIVEN TO A TOP-SECRET MILITARY INSTALLATION..."
BLAM
WUP-WUP WUP-WUP
IT'S A BLOW-OUT, SIR! I'LL GET IT CHANGED AS SOON AS--HUH?!
THE ROADWAY'S BEEN COVERED WITH SOME SORT OF SPIKED BARBS!
HOLD IT RIGHT THERE, SOLDIER! ONE MOVE AND YOU WON'T LIVE TO SEE THE DAWN!
BAH! DO NOT WASTE YOUR TIME WITH THE ENLISTED MAN!
HUH?!
YES! SILENCE HIM AND SEIZE THE COLONEL--HE IS THE ONE WE WANT!
WAIT A MINUTE! YOU CAN'T--WHUNNGH!
DO NOT TELL US WHAT WE CANNOT DO!
YOU ARE COMING WITH US, COLONEL HENSON! THE FATHERLAND WISHES TO LEARN WHAT YOU KNOW!
EH?
VRRRRROOOM
THAT NOISE... WHAT--?
YOU'RE NOT TAKING ANYONE ANYWHERE, NAZI!
MEIN GOTT!

"ROGERS' REPORT ON THAT ENCOUNTER WAS QUITE MODEST, BUT FROM THE STATEMENT WHICH WAS LATER SUBMITTED BY COLONEL HENSON--
"--IT SOUNDS LIKE OUR SUPER-SOLDIER TORE INTO THOSE FIFTH COLUMNISTS LIKE A ONE-MAN ARMY!"
SCREE-VROOM
DROP THAT TOMMY-GUN, MISTER-- DROP IT!
YOU FELLOWS DON'T LISTEN VERY WELL, DO YOU? IF YOU'RE NOT GOING TO DROP THE GUN, I'LL HAVE TO DROP YOU!
WHUNK
LOOKS LIKE THAT TIP WHICH ARMY INTELLIGENCE RECEIVED, ABOUT A POSSIBLE ATTEMPT TO KIDNAP COLONEL HENSON, WAS ON THE UP-AND-UP AFTER ALL!
FOR THE LAST SEVERAL MILES, I'D THOUGHT THIS EVENING WAS GOING TO YIELD ME NOTHING MORE THAN A NICE RIDE IN THE NIGHT AIR!
OOK
ERK
WHU
IT IS NOT POSSIBLE! THE MAN ISN'T HUMAN!
YUNNNK
THAT'S WHERE YOU'RE WRONG!
I'M TOTALLY HUMAN! BUT I'M FIGHTING FOR A CAUSE... A DREAM! AND THAT MAKES ALL THE DIFFERENCE!

VERDAMMT FOOL! WE FIGHT FOR A CAUSE, AS WELL--THE CAUSE OF THE THIRD REICH!
YES, BUT YOUR CAUSE ISN'T A DREAM...IT'S A NIGHTMARE!
PTANG
PTING
BUDA-BUDA
AND DON'T FLATTER YOURSELF BY THINKING THAT YOU CAN STOP ME WITH THAT CHATTER-GUN!
IT WON'T DO YOU ANY MORE GOOD THAN IT DID YOUR PARTNER!
WUMP
BUDA-BUDA-BUDA
NOW, WHERE'S THAT LEADER OF YOURS?
NO, HE MUSTN'T CAPTURE ME! I MUST GET BACK TO BUND HEADQUARTERS, AND REPORT THIS TO MY SUPERIORS!
YOU'RE NOT GOING ANYWHERE, FRITZ!
WHUU--?!
WHIZZZ
YOU'RE NOT CAUSING ANY MORE TROUBLE TONIGHT!
WHAP
EEESH!

THAT... THAT WAS THE MOST AMAZING DISPLAY OF HAND-TO-HAND COMBAT I'VE EVER SEEN!
THANK YOU, SIR, BUT I WAS JUST DOING MY JOB...KEEPING YOU AND THE NATION SAFE!
YOU CERTAINLY DO YOUR JOB VERY WELL, SON. BUT WHO IN BLAZES ARE YOU?!
WHO I AM DOESN'T MATTER, SIR... BUT YOU CAN CALL ME CAPTAIN AMERICA!
AND NOW, IF YOU'LL EXCUSE ME, I THINK G-2 WILL WANT TO ASK THIS GENTLEMAN SOME QUESTIONS!
COLONEL? WHO WAS THAT MASKED MAN?
LIKE HE SAID, CORPORAL, IT DOESN'T MATTER!
"TWENTY-FOUR HOURS LATER, ALARMED BY THE FAILURE OF THEIR ATTACK SQUAD TO REPORT IN, MAJOR NAZI BUND LEADERS MET IN A SECLUDED NEW YORK WAREHOUSE--
"--WITH A RECENT ARRIVAL FROM OVERSEAS!"
THE FUEHRER WILL NOT BE PLEASED BY THIS FAILURE!
W-WE QUITE UNDERSTAND, HERR KLEIN-SCHMIDT. WE CAN'T FIGURE OUT WHAT WENT WRONG!
HOWEVER, WE HAVE HEARD RUMORS OF SOME NEW GOVERNMENT SUPER-AGENT--!
KRASH
AND HERE'S WHERE THOSE RUMORS GET CONFIRMED!

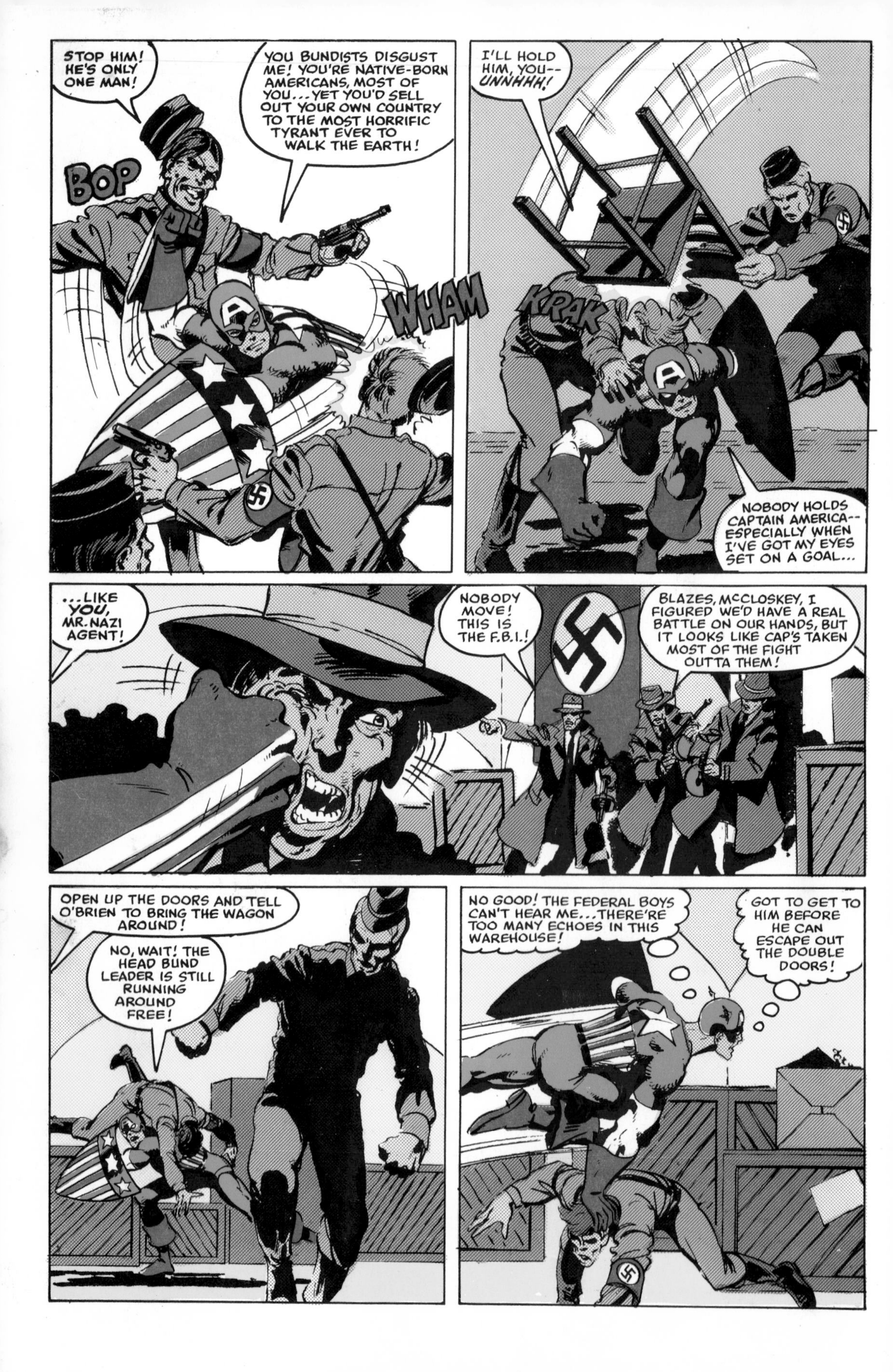
STOP HIM! HE'S ONLY ONE MAN!
YOU BUNDISTS DISGUST ME! YOU'RE NATIVE-BORN AMERICANS, MOST OF YOU... YET YOU'D SELL OUT YOUR OWN COUNTRY TO THE MOST HORRIFIC TYRANT EVER TO WALK THE EARTH!
BOP
WHAM
I'LL HOLD HIM, YOU-- UNNHHH!
KRAK
NOBODY HOLDS CAPTAIN AMERICA-- ESPECIALLY WHEN I'VE GOT MY EYES SET ON A GOAL...
...LIKE YOU, MR. NAZI AGENT!
NOBODY MOVE! THIS IS THE F.B.I.!
BLAZES, McCLOSKEY, I FIGURED WE'D HAVE A REAL BATTLE ON OUR HANDS, BUT IT LOOKS LIKE CAP'S TAKEN MOST OF THE FIGHT OUTTA THEM!
OPEN UP THE DOORS AND TELL O'BRIEN TO BRING THE WAGON AROUND!
NO, WAIT! THE HEAD BUND LEADER IS STILL RUNNING AROUND FREE!
NO GOOD! THE FEDERAL BOYS CAN'T HEAR ME... THERE'RE TOO MANY ECHOES IN THIS WAREHOUSE!
GOT TO GET TO HIM BEFORE HE CAN ESCAPE OUT THE DOUBLE DOORS!

WELL! I'M IN LUCK... IN HIS PANIC, HE RAN RIGHT PAST A POSSIBLE ESCAPE ROUTE!
I'M CALLING A HALT TO THIS BEFORE SOME INNOCENT BYSTANDER GETS HURT!
COME ON, MISTER, ALL YOU CAN DO NOW IS SURRENDER! NOTHING IN THAT PILE OF SCRAP METAL WILL HELP YOU.
YOU THINK SO, DO YOU?
WHAT'S GOING ON IN HERE?
"THE YOUNG NEWSPAPERMAN'S SHOUT MIGHT HAVE DISTRACTED ANOTHER MAN, BUT NOT CAPTAIN AMERICA! HOWEVER..."
THE MINIONS OF THE THIRD REICH SHALL NEVER FALL! THE REICH SHALL LAST A THOUSAND YEARS!
HEIL HITLER!
HE TELEGRAPHED THAT SWING BY A MILE! IT WAS EASY TO DUCK, BUT HE CAUGHT ONE OF THE WING-TIPS OF MY MASK... KNOCKED IT AJAR!
HEY! YOU WITH THE MASK... HOLD IT!
SORRY, NO TIME FOR THAT NOW!
THAT WAS CLOSE!
IT WOULDN'T DO FOR MY FACE TO BE PHOTOGRAPHED... THAT WOULD DESTROY MY EFFECTIVENESS AS AN ANONYMOUS SYMBOL!
I HAVE TO GIVE SOME THOUGHT TO REDESIGNING MY MASK, SO THIS CAN'T HAPPEN AGAIN!
THIS IS THE LAST OF THEM, AGENT McCLOSKEY!
THANKS FOR THE HELP, CAP! IF WE HAD A FEW MORE AGENTS LIKE YOU, WE COULD REDUCE ESPIONAGE BY A THIRD!
"THE INFORMATION GATHERED IN THAT RAID DEALT A SEVERE BLOW TO NAZI FIFTH COLUMN ACTIVITIES, MR. PRESIDENT--"

--AND HELPED CAPTAIN AMERICA TO SHUT DOWN A NUMBER OF SPY RINGS! IT'S ALL THERE IN THE DOSSIER.
MARVELOUS! I'M GRATIFIED TO SEE THAT THE ACTIVITIES OF OUR CAPTAIN HAVE BEEN SO WELL DOCUMENTED. THIS ENTRY, FOR EXAMPLE--
"--DEALING WITH THE ATTEMPTED THEFT OF A NEW BOMB-SIGHT FROM THE GRUMMAN AIRCRAFT PLANT!
"THREE AXIS AGENTS HAD GAINED ENTRY, DISGUISED AS ARMED FORCES PERSONNEL.
"BUT..."
YOU MIGHT HAVE FOOLED THOSE GUARDS AT THE GATE, BUT YOU DIDN'T FOOL ME, 'MAJOR'!
EVEN IF I HADN'T BEEN TAILING YOUR LITTLE CREW FOR THESE PAST THREE HOURS...THOSE SHOES YOU'RE WEARING WOULD HAVE BEEN A DEAD GIVEAWAY!
THEY'RE HARDLY REGULATION FOOTWEAR!
ACH!
AND AS FOR THESE PHONY 'AIDES' OF YOURS--!
BAM
WUD
"IN LESS THAN A MINUTE, CAPTAIN AMERICA HAD ENDED ALL ENEMY RESISTANCE AND DISAPPEARED INTO THE NIGHT, LEAVING THREE BEDRAGGLED SPIES BEHIND FOR THE MILITARY POLICE TO CART AWAY.

"TWO WEEKS LATER, AT ANOTHER IMPORTANT INSTALLATION..."
LIBERTY SHIP-YARDS
QUICKLY... BEFORE ANYONE SEES YOU!
DO NOT WORRY, MY FRIEND, BY THE TIME ANYONE IS AROUND TO SEE ANYTHING, IT WILL BE TOO LATE!
VERY WELL... IN HERE! HURRY!
"SECONDS LATER..."
THERE, THE EXPLOSIVE CHARGE IS IN PLACE! WHEN THE ASSEMBLY LINES START TO RUN TOMORROW, THIS ENTIRE FACTORY WILL BE LEVELED!
AH... AH... AH...
YES? WHAT IS IT?
"AND FINALLY, JUST LAST WEEK, FOLLOWING INFORMATION GATHERED BY THE F.B.I. AND G-2, CAPTAIN AMERICA STOPPED ONE OF THE MOST INCREDIBLE PLOTS EVER SET IN MOTION AGAINST THIS NATION IN PEACETIME--
"--THE ATTEMPTED DESTRUCTION OF BOULDER DAM!"
"DISGUISED AS MAINTENANCE MEN, THREE SABOTEURS WERE CAUGHT RED-HANDED, SETTING HIGH-EXPLOSIVE CHARGES IN THE MIGHTY TURBINE GENERATORS OF THE DAM'S HYDRO-ELECTRIC PLANT!
"AGAINST AMERICA'S SUPER-SOLDIER--
"--THEY NEVER HAD A CHANCE!
WAMM
"WERE IT NOT FOR CAPTAIN AMERICA, THIS NATION WOULD HAVE LOST AN IMPORTANT SOURCE OF WATER AND ELECTRICAL POWER. WE OWE THAT MAN A GREAT DEAL--"

--AND I HAVE LITTLE DOUBT THAT, BEFORE THE INTERNATIONAL AFFAIRS OF MAN ARE ONCE AGAIN PUT IN ORDER, WE WILL BE EVEN MORE IN HIS DEBT!
WELL, WHEN DO I GET TO MEET OUR SUPER-SOLDIER?
RIGHT AWAY, SIR!
CAPTAIN--!
THE DOOR TO THE OVAL OFFICE SWINGS WIDE, AND...
GOOD MORNING, MR. PRESIDENT. THIS IS A GREAT HONOR!
YOUR FIRE-SIDE CHATS ON THE RADIO HAVE BEEN AN INSPIRATION TO US ALL.
THANK YOU, SON, BUT I DARE SAY I'M NOT THE ONLY ONE PRESENT IN THIS OFFICE WHO'S BEEN AN INSPIRA-TION.
AS A MATTER OF FACT, I'VE READ MORE ABOUT YOU IN THE PAPERS LATELY, THAN I HAVE ABOUT *ME!*
GOOD THING THIS ISN'T AN ELECTION YEAR, EH?
I SEE THAT ARMY ORDNANCE HAS FINALLY MADE THE ALTERATIONS IN YOUR UNIFORM.
YES, SIR, MR. PRESIDENT. I WON'T HAVE TO WORRY ABOUT LOSING MY MASK IN BATTLE ANY LONGER... AND THE ADDED DURALUMIN CHAIN-MAIL PROVIDES EXCELLENT PROTECTION FOR MY NECK!
YES, WELL, I HAVE ANOTHER LITTLE ADDITION FOR YOUR BATTLE GEAR.
A NEW SHIELD! IT'S... MAGNIFICENT! IT'S MUCH LIGHTER THAN MY OLD SHIELD. AND WITH ITS DISCUS-LIKE SHAPE, I'LL BE ABLE TO HURL IT TWICE AS FAR!
IT SHOULD BE AS EFFECTIVE AN OFFENSIVE WEAPON AS A DEFENSIVE ONE! I ASSUME IT'S AS BULLETPROOF AS MY OLD SHIELD?
EVEN MORE SO! IN FACT, I'M TOLD THAT THE METAL IN THE SHIELD HAS SOME INCREDIBLE PROPERTIES.
IF ONLY THE METALUR-GICAL ACCIDENT WHICH PRODUCED IT COULD BE DUPLICATED...
AH, BUT THIS IS NO TIME FOR RE-CRIMINATIONS! CAPTAIN, ARE YOU READY FOR THE SECOND PHASE OF PROJECT: SUPER-SOLDIER?
SIR, I'M READY FOR ANYTHING.
SPLENDID! THE ARMY HAS DEVISED A PLAN TO ENABLE YOU TO MOVE ABOUT IN SECRET, BUT STILL BE CLOSE BY FOR SPECIAL MISSIONS. WE'RE GOING TO GIVE YOU A COVER IDENTITY...

JULY, 1941... CAMP LEHIGH.
STEVE ROGERS...NOW PRIVATE STEVE ROGERS...ADJUSTS TO THE ROUTINE OF ARMY BOOT CAMP...
ROGERS, YOU MEATHEAD, IS THAT THE ONLY POSITION YOU KNOW?
NO, SIR. WHAT POSITION DO YOU WANT?
NO TALKING AT ATTENTION! I DO THE TALKING! NOW...
...PARAAADE REST!
OWWW! NOT ON MY FOOT, YOU @☆xx!@!x IDJIT!
UH-OH.
@XX☆!!6XX! WHY? WHY, OF ALL THE SERGEANTS IN THIS MAN'S ARMY, DID I GET STUCK WITH A FUMBLE-BUTT LIKE YOU?!
GEE, I DON'T KNOW, SARGE. I...
ROGERS
SHADDAP!
JUST THEN...
HEY, SARGE! COLONEL FEENEY WANTS TO SEE YA OVER AT H.Q.
YEAH? THANKS, BARNES!
YOU GET OFF LUCKY THIS TIME, ROGERS!
DIS-MISSED!
SGT. DUFFY IS REALLY AN ALL-RIGHT JOE. I HATE TO GIVE HIM A HARD TIME, BUT THE PENTAGON WANTS ME TO PLAY THE CLUMSY RECRUIT... SO NO ONE WILL SUSPECT ME OF BEING CAPTAIN AMERICA.
I'D STAY OUTTA HIS WAY FOR A WHILE, STEVE! HE'S GONNA BE EVEN MADDER WHEN HE FINDS OUT THERE AIN'T NO COLONEL FEENEY!
WHAT? THERE ISN'T?
NAW! I JUST FIGURED YOU COULD USE A BREATHER FROM THAT CHEWIN' OUT, AND HE WON'T PICK ON ME! HECK, EVER SINCE MY OLD MAN DIED IN BASIC TRAINING, AND I WAS ADOPTED AS CAMP MASCOT, I CAN GET AWAY WITH JUST ABOUT ANYTHING!
WELL, I APPRECIATE THE FAVOR, BUCKY. C'MON, AND I'LL BUY YOU A COKE AT THE P.X.
GEE, THANKS, STEVE! SAY, DIDJA READ THE LATEST ABOUT CAPTAIN AMERICA?
NO. WHAT'S HE UP TO NOW?
2ND INF BN
HE BROKE UP ANOTHER NEST OF NAZI SPIES!
BOY, WOULDN'T IT BE GREAT TO HAVE A GUY LIKE HIM AROUND?
AW, WHO NEEDS 'IM, BUCK? YOU'VE GOT ME, HAVEN'T YOU?
WOTTA GUY! YOU'RE ALWAYS CLOWNIN', STEVE!
POST-COURIER
CAPTAIN AMERICA NABS SPY RING

BUT ONE NIGHT, JUST A FEW MONTHS LATER, YOUNG JAMES BUCHANAN BARNES STUMBLED ACROSS ONE OF HIS NATION'S MOST GUARDED SECRETS, AND CHANGED HIS LIFE FOR ALL TIME!
PLEDGING TO KEEP STEVE'S SECRET, BUCKY UNDERWENT MONTHS OF INTENSIVE TRAINING, BECOMING CAP'S PARTNER IN THE WAR AGAINST TYRANNY!
THEN CAME THAT AWFUL DAY... DECEMBER 7th, 1941. AND AMERICA WAS TRULY AT WAR!
BEFORE THE YEAR HAD ENDED, CAP AND BUCKY FOUND THEMSELVES ALLIED WITH A GROUP OF POWERFUL BEINGS... A SUPER-TEAM WHICH WINSTON CHURCHILL DUBBED THE INVADERS!
FOR FOUR INCREDIBLE YEARS, THEY BATTLED THE NAZI MENACE--
--IN ALL OF ITS BIZARRE FORMS!

THEN, IN THE WAR'S FINAL DAYS, TRAGEDY STRUCK AGAIN! WHILE TRYING TO STOP A RUNAWAY, EXPERIMENTAL DRONE PLANE, CAP AND BUCKY WERE CAUGHT ON THE SPEEDING CRAFT AS IT HEADED OUT OVER THE NORTH ATLANTIC.
SUDDENLY, THE PLANE EXPLODED! BUCKY WAS KILLED INSTANTLY, BUT CAP WAS THROWN CLEAR OF THE EXPLOSION, PLUNGING INTO ICY ARCTIC WATERS.
THERE, THROUGH A FREAK ACCIDENT, HE WAS FROZEN INTO A STATE OF SUSPENDED ANIMATION. DECADES PASSED...
...AND FINALLY, CAP'S BODY WAS FOUND BY A NEW SUPER-TEAM WHICH HAD COME INTO BEING... A TEAM CALLED THE AVENGERS!
THEY VIEWED THEIR FIND WITH AWE, FOR MANY OF THE AVENGERS HAD FOUND INSPIRATION IN THE HISTORY-MAKING EXPLOITS OF THIS RED-WHITE-AND-BLUE LEGEND!
AND THEY WERE EVEN MORE AWED TO DISCOVER THAT CAP WAS NOT DEAD! THE LEGEND LIVED! AND HE SOON TOOK HIS PLACE AMONG THEM, OFTTIMES AS LEADER!
BUT STILL, EVEN AS AN AVENGER, HE WAS A MAN DECADES OUT OF TIME. AND IN THE MONTHS THAT FOLLOWED, STEVE ROGERS STROVE TO FIND A PLACE FOR HIMSELF IN THIS BRAVE NEW WORLD.
HE STROVE... AND SEARCHED... AND SUCCEEDED.

IN CO
ESS. JULY 4, 1776.
The unanimous Declara
States of America.

And now we've come full circle. We've seen how Captain America came to be. We've seen his valiant battles against tyranny and injustice. We've seen how he survived across the years. And we've seen him take up the never-ending fight once more in our own era. Captain America's courage and spirit have been tested time and again. The legend *still* lives!

CAPTAIN AMERICA—LOOKING TO THE FUTURE!

America is at a great crossroads. The world is not as simple as it used to be. Maybe it never was as simple as it seemed. But evil is no longer as easy to recognize as it was when we were faced with a nation of inhumane Nazis. Today events are faster-paced and more complex.

Captain America knows that the situation in the world is different now. And he knows that to be a symbol of America, he must also be a symbol of the times. But one thing doesn't change. Captain America believes in people. He believes that human dignity and human liberty are precious.

To keep in touch, Captain America is spending less of his "free time" at Avengers Mansion. Instead, Steve Rogers is living in a rooming house in Brooklyn. He has developed his artistic talents into a full-fledged career. Unlike most jobs, being a freelance artist allows Steve to keep his own hours. He needs that sort of flexibility to operate effectively as Captain America.

Finally, it is Captain America's ability to think, search, and question that has made him a legend. He does not spout slogans. He lives what he believes. One could hardly expect less from a legend!

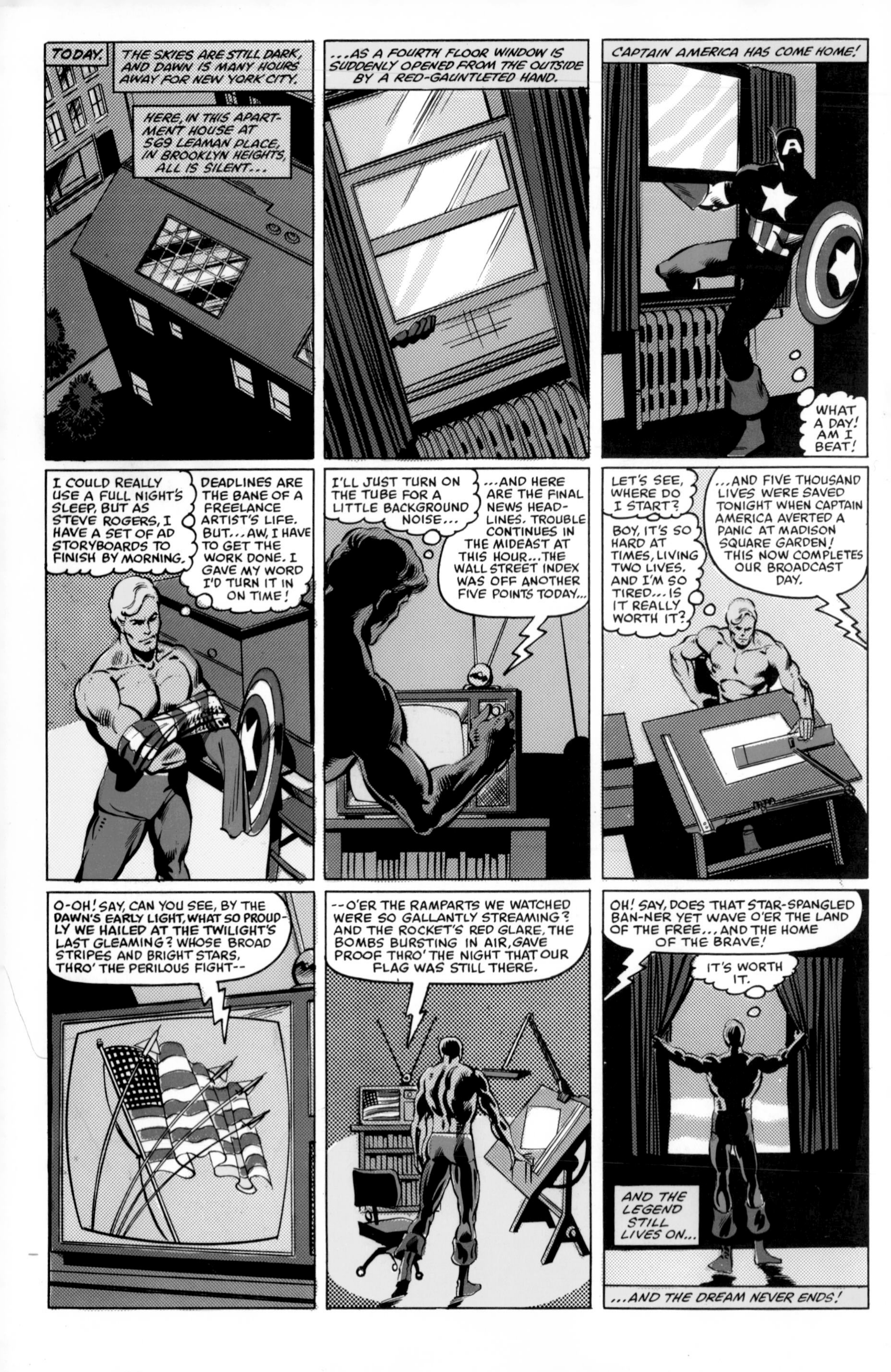
TODAY.
THE SKIES ARE STILL DARK, AND DAWN IS MANY HOURS AWAY FOR NEW YORK CITY.
HERE, IN THIS APARTMENT HOUSE AT 569 LEAMAN PLACE, IN BROOKLYN HEIGHTS, ALL IS SILENT...
...AS A FOURTH FLOOR WINDOW IS SUDDENLY OPENED FROM THE OUTSIDE BY A RED-GAUNTLETED HAND.
CAPTAIN AMERICA HAS COME HOME!
WHAT A DAY! AM I BEAT!
I COULD REALLY USE A FULL NIGHT'S SLEEP, BUT AS STEVE ROGERS, I HAVE A SET OF AD STORYBOARDS TO FINISH BY MORNING.
DEADLINES ARE THE BANE OF A FREELANCE ARTIST'S LIFE. BUT... AW, I HAVE TO GET THE WORK DONE. I GAVE MY WORD I'D TURN IT IN ON TIME!
I'LL JUST TURN ON THE TUBE FOR A LITTLE BACKGROUND NOISE...
...AND HERE ARE THE FINAL NEWS HEADLINES. TROUBLE CONTINUES IN THE MIDEAST AT THIS HOUR... THE WALL STREET INDEX WAS OFF ANOTHER FIVE POINTS TODAY...
LET'S SEE, WHERE DO I START?
BOY, IT'S SO HARD AT TIMES, LIVING TWO LIVES. AND I'M SO TIRED... IS IT REALLY WORTH IT?
...AND FIVE THOUSAND LIVES WERE SAVED TONIGHT WHEN CAPTAIN AMERICA AVERTED A PANIC AT MADISON SQUARE GARDEN! THIS NOW COMPLETES OUR BROADCAST DAY.
O-OH! SAY, CAN YOU SEE, BY THE DAWN'S EARLY LIGHT, WHAT SO PROUDLY WE HAILED AT THE TWILIGHT'S LAST GLEAMING? WHOSE BROAD STRIPES AND BRIGHT STARS, THRO' THE PERILOUS FIGHT--
--O'ER THE RAMPARTS WE WATCHED WERE SO GALLANTLY STREAMING? AND THE ROCKET'S RED GLARE, THE BOMBS BURSTING IN AIR, GAVE PROOF THRO' THE NIGHT THAT OUR FLAG WAS STILL THERE.
OH! SAY, DOES THAT STAR-SPANGLED BAN-NER YET WAVE O'ER THE LAND OF THE FREE... AND THE HOME OF THE BRAVE!
IT'S WORTH IT.
AND THE LEGEND STILL LIVES ON...
...AND THE DREAM NEVER ENDS!

NOW YOU KNOW...

If you have read this amazing book carefully, you now know the answers to these questions about our star-spangled hero, Captain America.

When did Captain America first begin his fight against oppression?

Why was he created at that time in history?

Who was Captain America's first sidekick and why isn't he with Cap in modern times?

What ideals does Captain America stand for?

Who discovered the Red Skull as a young man and why did he decide to turn him into a force for evil?

How did Captain America and the Red Skull survive until modern times?

What evil secret organization discovered the Red Skull and set him free?

Why do you think fate enabled Captain America to survive over the years and what was his mission?

What was unusual about Batrok the Leaper?

Are the Avengers friends or foes of Captain America?

Who is Captain America's most recent partner and what happened to him at the hands of the Red Skull?

Where does Captain America live now and what does he do for a living?

CAN YOU GUESS?...

Do you think there will *ever* come a time when Captain America's services are no longer needed in this world?

What do you think would have to happen before the world could manage without the likes of our star-spangled friend?

THE MEN BEHIND CAPTAIN AMERICA!

JOE SIMON AND JACK KIRBY

These two men, together, shaped the golden age of comics in the 1940s. Their list of credits reads like a who's who of classic comic-book heroes. They worked together during most of the forties, before Jack began moving in other directions. Eventually, of course, Jack teamed up with Stan Lee. Together, with a small group of other artists, they created Marvel Comics. Maybe you've heard of them. The rest, as they say, is history.

STAN LEE

Stan is the publisher and driving force behind Marvel Comics. In the early sixties, he was editor and head writer. With the help of a small group of talented artists, Stan created the Marvel Age of Comics. He created the Fantastic Four, Spider-Man, the Hulk, and many others. But one of his fondest memories was of a red-white-and-blue avenger from his youth—Captain America. In fact, the first story he ever sold was a Captain America story. Stan decided to bring the living legend of the golden age into the Marvel age.

Many talented artists and writers have assisted and contributed to making this legend live again. Foremost are **Roger Stern**, writer, and **John Byrne**, artist. The origin story in this volume was impressively told by these two, based on conceptions by Joe, Jack, and Stan. Roger and John are two of the most talented new members of the Marvel team. There is no doubt that these two will be creating their own "living legends" in their time.